I

THE
MEDICAL
SUPREME
COURT

THE
MEDICAL
SUPREME
COURT

PETE GRANT

NEWMARK PUBLISHING COMPANY

Published in 2001 by
Newmark Publishing Company
South Windsor, Connecticut 06074
Phone or fax (860) 282-7265

Designed by Newmark Publishing
Manufactured in the United States of America

10 9 8 7 6 5 4 3 2 1

Library of Congress Control Number: 2001 131121

Grant, Pete
The Medical Supreme Court
1. Second Constitutional Convention with changes to the Constitution. 2. A
Medical Supreme Court. 3. Malpractice case studies for breast, ovary and prostate. 4. Disability of the President, Vice President, Congress and the Supreme
Court. 5. Term limits for Congress. 6. Rights to privacy, due process and
equal protection under the law. 7. Campaign finance reform -- limits on expenditures.

ISBN 0-938539-16-7

AUTHOR'S NOTE

This book is a work of political and medical fiction. The author has been a medical expert witness in some of the case studies presented and the names, locales, and contents have been altered to improve interest and to protect the confidentiality of the patients. If there are any inaccuracies, they should be considered fictional additions. Any references to real events, businesses, organizations and media are intended only to help give the story a sense of reality.

EPIGRAPH

Do you rulers indeed speak justly?
Do you judge uprightly among men?

Psalm 58:1

How long will you defend the unjust and show partiality to the wicked?

Psalm 82:2

Rise up, oh judge of earth; pay back to the proud what they deserve.

Psalm 94:2

DEDICATION

This book is dedicated to my wife Barbara and our children: Kathy, Steve, Suzanne and Carolyn.

PROLOGUE

Thomas Jefferson Whitehall, a most unlikely name for a prominent American conspirator, had traveled a long, tedious way to get to Peshawar, Pakistan, just thirteen miles from the Khyber Pass, the most famous pass in the world. It lies along the border between Pakistan and Afghanistan. From Turkey to China, Peshawar is called "the city of central Asia." The climate is extreme here, intensely hot, dry summers and bitterly cold winters. Peshawar is known for the people who have visited it; Marco Polo, Alexander the Great, Emperors Babus and Akbar, Lawrence of Arabia, Queen Elizabeth II of England, and many others. It's one of the cities of the ancient world, a city of intrigue, mystery, violence and spies – people pretending to be someone they aren't. Thomas Jefferson Whitehall easily fit that description. He had flown into the Karachi Airport on British Airways, took a PIA commuter flight to Peshawar, and was looking for the University Compound and the Jihad.

Tom had been a member of one of the brigades of the Montana militia back in the U.S.A. that had been involved in the S.A.M. attack on former President Diamond's plane and the launching of the cruise missile at the White House. He missed the major event in Maryland and Washington D.C., but because he was one of the individuals involved in the conspiracy to destroy the American government as it existed, and had been one of the militia's frequent spokesmen, he was sentenced to three years in prison at hard labor in Georgia. The summer heat and workload was suffocating there and it left a permanent imprint in his brain. He was now out and looking for revenge. Beneath the mirage of his collected poise was a cauldron of vengeance, ready to explode. Not only was he paranoid, he was bordering on a schizoid character disorder that sometimes became uncontrollable. When those missiles went off over Washington, D.C., the mission was to destroy the White House and the U.S. government. Thirty of his surviving co-conspirators had been executed or had received life imprisonment. He actually still believed there were people in the government of the United States who were involved in a secret plot to destroy it. The militia's failure to accomplish their mission only intensified the hatred boiling in Tom Whitehall's body. He was a sick American.

When his plane landed at Peshawar, he took a cab to the Old City and the Galaxy Hotel where he would be staying. It was a cheap hotel but it had air conditioning. The cost was nine American dollars a night.

He had traveled to Peshawar to get to the Northwest Frontier Province and to seek out the Islamic leaders in the gun factory areas of Darra Adam Khel. It is an extremely dangerous area to go to, since Pakistani laws don't apply. The main street is made up of gun shops including the Khyber Pass Armaments Company. A Darra gunsmith, given a rifle he's never seen before, can duplicate it in ten days and with the templates can duplicate the rifle in two or three days. Handguns take longer and the dealers will sell to anyone with the money. Guns disguised as pens or walking sticks can be purchased here – also anti-aircraft guns and the M-16 American made rifle.

Tom was not here to purchase guns, however, he was here to contact Islamic chiefs to solicit help in his efforts to get even and destroy the U.S. government.

Tom knew all about the Jihad. In the center of Darra, was a refugee camp, the home of the Islamic Alliance.

It was the training ground of Ramzi Ahmed Yousef, the mastermind for the bombing of the World Trade Center, who was sentenced to life imprisonment for his involvement. "Jihad" means holy war and Yousef was a perpetrator of a global "Jihad". Fanatic evolutionary powerful Afghan warlords who wanted to change the world's thinking led the school at the University.

Religious wars have been very common and dangerous, and Peshawar is very old, over 2000 years old and it has seen religions come and go. In the Seventh Century, Peshawar was the center of Buddhist Gaudharran civilization and a place of pilgrimage. Today, the Peshawar inhabitants have converted to Islam and worshipping idols has ceased. Buddhism is out.

The world has been affected by conspiracies for centuries. Part of the overall Islam plan is to destroy the Christian order of the Western nations and replace it with an atheistic socialistic one-world dominated by the Islamic leaders.

The Afghan's are now under the Taliban's Rule, which punished and still punishes adulterers and homosexuals with death by stoning. Thieves have their hands cut off, and girls and women are barred from business and school. They have to wear burkas, a head to toe loose garment and their faces have to be covered even as they work in the fields. They are debased and oppressed but they are not raped like in the past.

The Taliban are occupied by war, terrorism is part of their make-up. You either follow the dictates of the Koran or you don't survive.

One of the most sought after terrorist in the world was Osana Bin Laden who engineered the terrorist bombing of the U.S. Embassies in Kenya and Tanzania. He was an extremely wealthy man who hated the U.S.A., and funded the training of future terrorists. He was now in hiding, plotting more terrorist activities with his followers in Afghanistan and was protected by the Taliban faction.

Tom's serving time in prison in Georgia, because of his role in the Washington, D.C. missile attack on the White House, had only increased his paranoia and hate. The world was against him and he felt there was a conspiracy to do him in. When he had been a Lieutenant Colonel in the U.S. Army, he had planned to remain in the army's military service but was passed over for promotion, as he describes it, "by political maneuvering by the higher ups." He felt he got screwed royally and he planned to get even if it was the last thing he did.

His preparation for coming to Peshawar was extensive. He took night courses at the State University to learn how to speak the various languages he would encounter. There were two dozen languages spoken in Pakistan and Afghanistan. The main ones are Urdu, Sindhi, Punjabi, Pashto and Baluchi. He concentrated particularly on Pashto, the language that dominated this region of Pakistan and Afghanistan. English is still the language of the ruling elite – government, military and business personnel. However, there are over three hundred dialects that compound the problem of understanding. Tom also learned to speak Persian and tried to learn about some of the important customs of the Pakistani people. He wore clothes not to offend the deviant Muslims, loose, non revealing garments. He ate his food completely with his right hand. The left hand is considered unclean – you accept food and drink only with the right hand.

He allowed his beard to grow and respected their Islam religion. He did not walk in front of someone praying to Mecca. Tom was determined not to foul things up. He was here for a purpose and that was to try to form an alliance with the Islamic warlords and with what remained of the Montana militia that had now gone underground.

When he arrived at the gate of the refugee camp, there were numerous youthful guards with machine guns slung over their shoulders, and there were also numerous satellite and radar dishes rotating above the buildings. The top security guard had a cellular phone and was fluent in several languages. He obviously controlled who was admitted to the compound. Tom presented his credentials and was told to wait in a locked room next to the gate that had bars on the windows and a bathroom. Two hours later, he was escorted in to see the Brigade Commander, Abdurrah Muhammad Rashid, who had been educated in Great Britain and spoke fluent English.

"What brings a Montana militia man to Pakistan?" he asked.

"How did you know I was a Montana militia man? It wasn't in my credentials."

"It's my business to know everyone I see or deal with."

"I'm interested in discussing our common goals," replied Tom.

"What might they be?"

"A combined effort to overthrow the United States government."

Rashid sat back, raised his arms and smiled and then laughed. "Many nations and more prominent individuals than you have tried to do that! You must be dreaming, or you're having a fantasy hallucination or you're just out-right paranoid or stupid!"

"I'm dead serious," replied Tom.

"You will end up dead if you try to do what you have just suggested," replied Rashid.

"There are risks in everything we do in life. I realize it's not going to be an easy undertaking."

"The F.B.I., C.I.A., and military intelligence in the United States are the top of the line. They are a formidable foe."

"I have some ideas of how to bypass them and accomplish my goal," replied Tom.

"Why do you think we will join you?" asked Rashid.

"Because I think your Islamic revolutionists are just as mad as the Montana militia. The U.S.A. is out to destroy all terrorists. One of your Islamic brothers remains in a mid-western penitentiary and is dying there and others have joined him for life imprisonment… missiles were fired by the United States at Afghanistan training sites for terrorists and at Sudan chemical factories. Many of our Montana militia were killed in Maryland in the Washington, D.C. shootout and we both want revenge."

"How do you plan this so-called revenge?"

"Our plot is not too much different from the previous one. It has a little different twist to it, however. We were almost successful the last time, although that cruise missile we fired hit the State Department building instead of the White House. Unfortunately the President and Vice President weren't in it. We've added some other militia recruits from the military who are willing to help us, although it's for a price."

"Everything has a price attached to it," replied Rashid. "The C.I.A. and Saudi Arabians gave us the money and helped train our army of Islamic militants. It's ironic that some of the men they helped train are the ones working to destroy them. Many of the Islamic Jihad have an intense hatred for the United States."

"I know," said Tom. "That's why I'm here."

"Are you sure? I'm not so sure that's why you're here. You could be a counterespionage agent for the C.I.A. or F.B.I. In fact, we know that probably both of those agencies know you're here now!"

Tom thought about that. His life could be at risk if they thought he was a counterespionage agent. He had to choose his words properly in response to Rashid's statement.

"I wouldn't take the risk of being here if I was a counterespionage agent," Tom replied. "I respect your groups intelligence."

"I'm not so sure. You had a short sentence after that Washington, D.C. disaster – only three years. Maybe your life was spared as part of a plea-bargaining arrangement. Before we have any serious discussions, you'll have to meet with our senior Islamic council members. We also have our own intelligence network in our Islamic Alliance around the world. We knew you were coming. We knew how much time you served in prison. You've been checked out completely. We'll call you in a few days if we wish to discuss your plans with our Islamic intelligence group."

Two days later, Tom received a hand-delivered message at the Galaxy Hotel informing him about a meeting the next day. The message stated that Rashid's henchmen would pick him up.

He noticed the security was tighter as he entered a large conference room in the compound. There were armed guards everywhere. Rashid was there with seven other Islamic chiefs seated around a long table.

He was introduced to the Intelligence Chief of the Islam Alliance, Hussen Hasiv Haddad. He was a middle aged athletic-looking man with chiseled Arabic features and a black mustache. He had brilliant green penetrating eyes and spoke fluent English with an accent. He was obviously well educated and wore a pistol on his hip.

Tom was told to sit in an elevated chair, separate from the Islamic chiefs. After he was seated, Haddad spoke, in perfect English.

"Rashid has informed us that you are a member of the Montana Militia Group that perpetrated the missile attack on the President of the United States and the White House. Is that correct?"

"Yes."

"Why weren't you executed?"

"Because I was not bodily involved in the S.A.M. missile attack from Maryland. However, I took part in the planning stage."

"If you tried something like that in our country, after we had gotten all the essential information out of you, you would have been tortured, almost flogged to death, and your body would have been dragged through the streets. You would have been allowed to suffer without any food or water. It would have been a slow, painful death. You would then be chained to a pole in the square for the birds to eat. Your government is too lenient on traitors."

"I don't consider myself a traitor. I'm trying to help my government so the people have more say in how it's run."

"When someone tries to overthrow their government, that's being a traitor!"

"I don't think so," replied Tom. "When our government was started, a lot of patriotic lives were lost in fighting the British.

They were called traitors also. Nathan Hale is an example. George Washington, our first President would have been called a traitor."

"Yes, that's true. I can see how you think," replied Haddad.

For the next two hours Tom presented his plan for over-throwing the U.S. government with many intricate details. There were two young Islamic interpreters that spoke fluent English with a British accent.Each one of the seven Islamic chiefs had questions Tom had to answer and he had difficulty in answering some of them.

One of the Islamic chiefs, Omar Kiam, was particularly hard on him.

"You were a failure in your first attempt and I'm sure you are considered a traitor in your own country now. You could fail again. I'm surprised you're still alive."

"A democracy doesn't work that way," replied Tom.

"Yes, that's one of their weaknesses!"

The Intelligence Chief, Haddad, spoke up.

"Our Islamic Chief's Alliance will consider your proposi-tion in secret assembly, and then we will decide. Rashid will meet with you in a few days and give you our answer. You are excused," he said as he gestured with his arm for Tom to leave.

Tom was extremely nervous waiting to hear from the Islamic Chiefs. He stayed pretty much in the Galaxy Hotel but the food wasn't very good. He cautiously went out for lunch in a nearby restaurant, but as he stepped out on the streets, he was over-whelmed by children and women wearing black burkas, begging for money or food. The burkas covered the women from head to toe, so you couldn't see their face or body… one hand would be out-stretched from underneath the burka. In the restaurant he had difficulty in swallowing his food, for the poor beggars watched him eating through the glass windows. He had the eerie feeling that he was being watched constantly, but not just by women and children beggars but by potential assassins. He was frightened and felt his paranoia taking over.

It was an overwhelming, stressful week before Tom was called back to the University. Haddad was the only one present. This time he was seated in a large chair at the end of a long conference table and there were two armed guards with machine guns standing next to him. Tom was nervous and anxious, standing before him… sweat was pouring off his brow, and his hcart began beating fast. He also had a hollow feeling in the pit of his stomach and felt that he might be getting sick. Perhaps they would kill him. Life was cheap in Afghanistan. They could easily kill him if they wanted to, and no one would know it or care.

Haddad finally broke the silence and spoke: "Our council has listened to you and reviewed your intricate plot during this past week. We will contact you if we decide to consider your proposition. It may take several months or years, but you are not to contact us! We are going to check out your plan. If we find out that you are lying to us and that you are a C.I.A. spy, we will seek you out, and torture you, and destroy you and your family. I believe you have three children. Is that correct?'

"Yes, Sir."

"The way you will know that we are involved is this coin that I will give you."

Haddad put a silver coin on the table and a board was placed under it. One of the armed guards took out a cleaver and chopped the coin in two at an angle.

"The individual carrying the other half of this coin will be from the Islam Alliance. Whether you know it or not, you have been under our protective blanket since you arrived here. You might wonder about that. We know you are under surveillance by C.I.A. agents who are now in Peshawar. We will protect you until you board your plane back to the States but after that you are on your own. The C.I.A. may have a contract out on your life and may decide to kill you. They probably suspected why you came here so you may not get back to the States alive."

"I didn't think I was being followed, but I certainly thought about it. I appreciate your telling me."

"Usually the C.I.A. contracts out their killers. They don't do it directly themselves. It could be a Pakistani or European or Asian who may attempt to kill you. Do you carry a gun?"

"No. You know I can't carry a gun in a foreign country."

Haddad started to laugh. "Anyone can have a gun here. Do you have cash?"

"Yes," he replied.

"We make all sorts of guns here – almost a thousand a day. If you've got the money, you can get the gun. However, you can't carry a gun on an airplane. If you don't have a gun, how do you protect yourself?"

"I have a thin wooden knife I carry in my suitcase."

"That's useless," said Haddad with a mocking loud laugh. "You must be stupid! We have something, which may help you defend yourself. My aide will give it to you as you leave. You wear size eleven D shoes, don't you?"

"Yes. How did you know?"

Haddad waved his hand and pointed at his head. He got up and walked out of the room. When Tom Whitehall left, an aide gave him a pair of leather boots. They looked like ordinary boots, but the inside lining of one of the boots hid a small automatic pistol made completely out of plastic. It had a silencer on it and it had twelve small plastic bullets inside the chamber containing high explosive powder. An additional twelve bullets were on the side of his other boot. The boots and gun were obviously constructed to pass through a metal detector. The aide showed Tom how to load the pistol.

"Use these bullets wisely," said the aide. "It might help you get back to the States. We think you're a marked man. Our guards will escort you back to your hotel room."

Tom got into a cab and two guards carrying machine guns got into the cab with him. One sat next to him and one sat next to the cab driver. He started sweating profusely. Getting out of Peshawar safely was going to be a big problem.

When he got back to his hotel room at the Galaxy, he was hesitant to enter for fear that an assailant might be in his room. If he was in there, he'd shoot to kill. Tom pulled out his plastic gun, kicked the door open, and entered the room slowly.

The room was completely ransacked… his suitcase and all of his clothes were missing. Fortunately, he had carried his plane ticket and passport with him, and his money was in a belt and pocketbook under his clothes. The door was locked and there were no signs of forced entry. He wondered how they got into his room and then glanced at the open window at the far end. He walked over and looked out and saw a flash of light in the distance… instinctively he ducked and hit the deck, as a bullet zinged by him and struck the back wall. Haddad was right. He was a marked target all right and he was in big trouble. Someone was out to kill him before he got back to the States.

Haddad told him they would protect him until he got on the plane. Where the hell were they?

The only weapon he had was that plastic pistol he had taken out of his boot. Could it really shoot or would it blow up in his face? Could he trust Haddad?.. he decided to test fire the gun. He took three pillows off the bed, held the gun away from his body, and pulled the trigger aiming at the pillows. It fired perfectly.

He called the desk to tell them about being shot at and he was surprised by their answer.

"Do you want us to notify the police?"

God! What kind of an answer was that? How asinine can they be? "Forget it," he replied. "Reserve a cab for me at 6:30 A.M."

"There's one reserved for you already."

Hmmm. That's interesting. How was he to know whether the Islamic Alliance had reserved a cab or if it was a trap?

In the morning, he would be taking a cab up the Khyber Road to the airport. His commuter flight would go to Karachi, where he would catch an international flight on British Airways to Frankfort and then on to New York City. Someone knew what room he was in, and was out to get him. He pushed a large wooden clothes cabinet in front of the balcony window, and then pushed the bed in front of the door. He decided to sit on the floor all night with his loaded gun, watching for any attempt at entry.

At 5:30 A.M. he went down to the lobby of the Galaxy Hotel and checked out, using his American Express credit card. The desk clerk informed him that the cab he ordered was waiting for him outside.

When he stepped out of the lobby to the street, a cab driver pointed to his cab.

"Mr. Whitehall, your cab is waiting," he said as he opened the car door.

"I've made other arrangements," replied Tom, noting that the cab driver wore a sidearm and knew his name.

"You must take my cab," he said. "I'm first in line."

"No way," Tom replied, as he walked to the second cab and quickly opened the door and stepped in. He pulled out two gold coins and showed them to the driver.

"These two gold coins are yours if you go as fast as you can to the airport and get me there safely."

"You got it, mister," he said in broken English as he jammed his foot down on the gas pedal and took off.

Tom looked through the back window of the cab, and saw the first cab driver trying to catch up to them.

"Step on that gas or you don't get those gold coins," he hollered at the cab driver."

"My cab is much faster than the one behind us. Just watch."

Sure enough. The dust began to fly behind them. Tom's cab lengthened the distance between them, burning rubber, and the other cab was nowhere in sight when they got to the airport.

He gave the two gold coins to the cab driver, jumped out and ran into the airport building. Inside there were armed policemen, so he felt somewhat secure. He located the waiting area for his commuter flight and checked in. Finally, the flight was called over the loudspeaker to board the plane going to Karachi.

Once he got into the plane, he breathed a sigh of relief, and then looked at the other passengers. He couldn't help but feel that they all looked like a bunch of crooks or felons that would kill for money.

Although he was tired, he was afraid to close his eyes on the long commuter flight from Peshawar.

When the plane landed in Karachi, Tom went to the British Airways ticket counter to check on his flight to Frankfort. His ticket and passport was in order and he had a couple of hours to wait. He noted that two of the Arabs on the flight from Peshawar seemed to be keeping an eye on him, and sat down in his section. Were they protecting him, were they out to kill him, or was his paranoia taking over? He tried to reassure himself that just because those two creepy characters were Arabs, it didn't mean that they were criminals out to get him. However, they certainly looked rugged, and capable of violence.

Added to his problems, was the fact that he hadn't gone to the bathroom for a couple of days because of the intense stress… He felt the urge to go and didn't like going to the bathroom on airplanes. Finally, he heard the announcement on the loudspeaker calling for the first class passengers to board his flight... He noticed that a large 777 Boeing had just pulled into the next bay, and passengers were disembarking, filling up the aisle along the waiting area.

He decided he better go… so he made a mad dash across the hall through the crowd to the bathroom, opened the door to a stall, sat on the john and had immediate relief. A few moments later, as he looked through the cracks, he saw the two Arabs that had been watching him enter the men's room… one was carrying a gun. Tom quickly took his plastic gun from his boot, wrapped toilet tissue around it and raised his feet so that he couldn't be seen. The Arabs started opening the stalls, one by one, and then opened his stall. Tom fired the pistol at the Arab with the gun and then fired two shots at the second Arab. They both fell to the floor.

Not a sound was heard because of the silencer. There was a whoosh, then a thud, and then a gasp by one of the victims, as the blood erupted. Two other occupants in the bathroom saw the shooting... they screamed.

Tom pulled up his pants, tightened his belt, and ran as fast as he could to the boarding site, shoving people out of his way as he scrambled aboard. The plane was finally loaded and ten minutes later it left the gate. When the plane got out to the end of the runway for take-off, it taxied off to one side. Tom's heart was in his throat as police came out and boarded the plane. They walked past him down the aisle in the first class section and handcuffed two Arabs in the back of the plane. Until the police got off the plane, the sweat really dripped from Tom's face.Once the big jet got into the air, he called the stewardess over and requested a double martini.

"You must have had a tough day," she remarked as she served him the drink.

"You'll never know how tough it was," he remarked. "Getting out of that airport saved my life."

Tom had another extra-dry martini on the flight to Frankfort and then boarded the plane to the States. However, he slept with one eye open.

AT THE WHITE HOUSE

President Kelli Palmer and members of the Joint Intelligence Committee of the House of Representatives and the Senate met for breakfast once a month. Also present, were the F.B.I. Chief, Mark Lynch, the Attorney General Tom Morris, and the

C.I.A. Chief Richard Deckers, who was sometimes referred to as "Big Dick", because of his overwhelming size and dominant characteristics. They briefed the President on sensitive intelligence problems in the domestic area and around the world. Kelli insisted on knowing what was going on and made sure the briefing by her staff was complete. If she knew something they didn't know, they were in big trouble, and she wasn't afraid to admonish them in front of the group.

The routine briefings by the F.B.I. and Attorney General seemed like everything was okay. Deckers got up to give his report concerning the worldwide activities of the C.I.A. He was in charge of the U.S.A. world involvement of covert operations... a real but ultra secretive part of our government's foreign operations. He dealt with life and death on a daily basis. Usually his report was longer than the rest. He touched on the various hot spots around the world and then Kelli would ask questions. First, he talked about the Middle East. Fortunately, Saddam Hussein was in bad health and a new regime of Iraq Generals had taken over.

A grandson, Hadaslin Sudan Hussein, was now the chief honcho and he was almost as bad as his grandfather. Rumors had it that Iraq now had nuclear bomb capabilities. All the countries in that area were continually bumping into each other about land control with frequent border clashes, and oil was still their claim to fame for supplying the world's energy.

Satellites monitored the activity of all the potentially suspect countries and these were interpreted daily by the military and C.I.A. agents looking for potential danger spots.

The United States had put up a missile defensive unit in one of the Aleutian Islands next to Alaska. This was upsetting China, who was trying to take control of the Far East and particularly the oil rich fields in Southeast Asia. Russia was also unhappy about the missile defensive unit.

Because of the missile attack on President Diamond's plane and the White House, the domestic area was discussed last, and usually Kelli was quite vehement about domestic security controls.

Air bases and S.A.M. missile sites had been increased around Washington, D.C. There was also secret underground construction going on for rapid evacuation of the White House and Capitol Congressional personnel.

C.I.A. Chief Deckers, briefly described all the activities around the world and then mentioned the loss of two C.I.A. agents in Peshawar, Pakistan.

"What's that all about?" asked Kelli.

"It's routine," replied Deckers.

"I'd like to hear about it."

"We were trying to eliminate a Montana militia man who was visiting the Islamic Alliance in Peshawar. Our information was that he was trying to form an alliance with the militia and the Islamic Alliance to try to destroy this country in some way. They're the ones who bombed the World Trade Center, Sudan, and numerous other areas."

"Are we sure about this?" asked Kelli.

"It's impossible to be sure about anything when it comes to spying," replied Deckers. "We have a mole in Peshawar, Pakistan, in the Islamic Alliance and that's what we were told.

"What happened was that we tried to bump off the militia man, but in the process, the Islamic Alliance Intelligence group killed our two agents first. What we don't like is that they were tortured in the public square and their bodies were hung in the streets so the people could see what happened with traitors. That's the way they handle spies."

"Is that all that happened?"

"To be honest, we lost two other men... hired killers. They followed the suspect to Karachi, and were found dead in the men's room at Karachi Airport."

"Who killed them?"

"We don't know."

"So you didn't accomplish what you set out to do, and lost four hired killers in the process. That's not good. Who authorized the killing and why was it authorized?"

"I did."

"In other words, you were going to assassinate this man; you authorized murder for hire. I'm sure you're aware of the Presidential executive order that states that no person employed by or acting on behalf of the United States Government shall engage in or conspire to engage in assassination. Wouldn't it have been better to keep that individual under surveillance to see what he was up to?"

"The C.I.A. thought it would be better to stop any merger between these two groups before anything bad happened. They could be plotting to destroy our country. We didn't want another missile attack at the White House."

"You're the director of the C.I.A. Did you approve it?"

"Yes."

"I'm not sure I approve of that. That activity was not discussed here."

"We can't discuss everything we do around the world. We could have moles within our own ranks."

"When it comes to taking a human life, I think we can. If the C.I.A. gets involved in killing, I want to know about it."

"There's no way I can keep you informed about everything!" Deckers said caustically.

Kelli had had it! She sensed insubordination and lit into Deckers.

"In the future, where human life may be at stake, the Secretary of State and myself are to be informed of that potential. Do you understand? Now the militia may be trying to do something in the future and they will be on the alert for our surveillance of their actions."

"Yes, Ms. President. It won't happen again."

"It better not!" replied Kelli.

Deckers was pissed off for the admonishment he received in front of the other senior members of the executive staff and congressmen, but there was nothing he could do about it. He had a very powerful job as Director of the C.I.A. with a tremendous budget and a great amount of influence. He didn't want to lose that. However, it was hard for him to take a bawling-out by a woman, and his face was beet red from embarrassment.

Kelli felt she had to do it. He was freewheeling without consent and he could be a loose cannon in the administration if she didn't rein him in.

The meeting ended on that note.

"You were tough on him," said Davis, her Chief of Staff.

"I had to be. The buck stops with me!"

Thomas Whitehall got back to the States safely, but in the process he had to kill two assassins. It was his life or theirs. He was lucky he got away with it. He decided he'd better stay underground for a while. There might be reprisals. He contacted one of the senior members of the militia and told him what had happened.

"You're lucky you're still alive. The F.B.I. or the C.I.A. will be watching you like a hawk In fact, they may try to bump you off again."

"I know."

"You're going to be under surveillance for quite awhile. I don't think I should meet with you."

"I agree. Why don't we use the secret code we set up to communicate on the Internet."

"Someone might break the code."

"We have twenty-six different codes. Why don't you use a different code each time? It will be hard to break, if they're all different."

"Okay, we'll try it. However, I'll contact you directly if the Islamic Alliance contacts me. There are twenty-six letters in the alphabet. The last letter on the message will tell you which one of the twenty-six codes I'll use."

PART ONE

1

PRESIDENT KELLI PALMER
STATE OF THE UNION ADDRESS

The Sergeant-at-Arms with his ceremonial mace, entered through the back door of the Capitol's chambers and loudly announced, "Hear Ye, Hear Ye, the President of the United States." All the members of the House, the Senate, and invited guests in the galleries stood up as President Kelli Palmer, dressed in a dark blue suit-dress with a white blouse, walked behind the Sergeant at Arms to the podium and dais. She shook the hands of the Congressmen as she walked by. Kelli held her head high, her red hair glistening in the bright lights. The people in the chambers continued to stand with sustained applause. This was indeed a memorial date to be remembered for posterity in the history books about the United States of America.

Kelli Fitzgerald Palmer was the first woman to be elected President. Television, radio, the news media from around the world, America-On-Line, and others were all present in force to document the event. The entire world was watching. What would this young woman with a confident and engaging warm smile have to say?

Kelli had speechwriters, but for this momentous occasion, she insisted on writing her own speech. It would be brief, but to the point.

The Speaker of the House continued to pound the gavel without response. Finally, the crowd stopped clapping and sat down, and then the Speaker of the House announced:

"The President of the United States, Kelli Fitzgerald Palmer..." all the people in the chambers stood up again and clapped for another long period of time. Finally, the applause stopped, and Kelli began to speak:

"Mr. Speaker, members of Congress, and my fellow Americans, it is with deep humility and pride that I stand before you as the first woman to be elected President of this great nation..."

The audience stood up, and there was sustained, prolonged applause.

"Thomas Jefferson, one of our greatest Presidents, drafted the Declaration of Independence in the year 1776... He wrote: 'We hold these truths to be self evident, that all men are created equal, that they are endowed by their creator with certain unalienable rights, that among these are Life, Liberty, and the Pursuit of Happiness...' Our founding fathers, a diverse group of dedicated, intelligent men, signed that document, and led by George Washington, fought and won our freedom. They were able to compromise their differences of opinion and establish a document, the Constitution that has withstood the passage of time. I stand before you now, as your President and as a woman, a milestone in this country's history, a symbol in restoring equality for all. I invite the Congress to come together with me in the process of governing, to show the

world what a democracy can do to help its people achieve a maturity that the world will respect.

I will present to Congress, new issues that need to be addressed, and several old issues that have been in a quagmire of controversy that has to be resolved. Resolving our differences is necessary for progress. Congress must learn to compromise and remain focused on the most important issues at hand. Bipartisan cohesion is necessary to succeed... Join with me in concert. Let us put our hands and minds together to accomplish our mutual goals.

First and foremost, we must achieve an excellent public education for all of our children, rich or poor. I am a product of public education, and I am proud of it! To use public taxes for vouchers for private schools is wrong because all students do not equally benefit. This is not meant to discourage private schools from existing, and competing.

The public school buildings should all be improved, particularly in the inner cities so that a healthy and safe environment will be conducive to the learning process. I endorse achievement tests for students and teachers, in order to maintain a high standard of education. I also endorse financial aid for a college education for students who need support and who stand in the upper twenty percent of their high school class." The children of today, are the leaders of tomorrow. We must educate them in order for this nation to survive and compete on the world's stage... the assembly stood up and there was prolonged applause.

"My second issue is health care, a perennial problem for all Americans. The health industry has grown more rapidly and costly. It is a big business that benefits the industry, but not always the patient. Doctor's costs have been controlled but administrative costs have escalated beyond comprehension. The administrators are getting bigger salaries than the doctors.

We have all forgotten that the doctors and the nurses are the backbone of all quality medical care and we have allowed big business and nonprofessional ancillary personnel to dictate to the doctors. Control of the patients should return to the doctors and the nurses where it belongs.

Affordable health care should be a privilege and a right, and everyone in this great wealthy country of ours, should have a basic coverage whether they can afford it or not. In order to accomplish this, I charge congress to appropriate funds for this purpose and to form a new separate Department of Health to oversee our health care system. Within the department there should be former practicing doctors who run the department and know healthcare issues and not an overabundance of administrative economic health gurus.

My third issue is the military defense budget. I have spent over twenty years in the Naval Air Corps to help maintain peace in the world. I strongly recommend that money for space technology be increased since the "Star Wars" concept of the future cannot be ignored.

I also recommend that we continue to develop a missile defense system for our country even if other nations object. We have been threatened with ballistic missiles on numerous occasions when we have intervened on the world stage. Terrorists around the world are becoming more active and unpredictable. Attempts must be made to control them. Chemical and biological warfare must also be addressed, and should be banned throughout the civilized world.

Last but not least, the fourth issue that congress must address is term limits for our congressmen. A constitutional amendment should be passed that will create term limits, six two year terms in the House, and three six year terms in the Senate.

Incumbents with seniority are destroying the will of the people. Their large campaign chests filled with funds make them impossible to defeat. Politicians, with the help of corporations, are buying elective offices at all levels. That's not what our forefathers contemplated. It is depriving the public of their individual voting rights. Funds for reelection should be obtained from the voters within their own state – the people they represent, not outside interests.

In closing, I would like the Congress to join with me in expressing a personal general commitment:

God, please give us the strength and intellectual foresight and fortitude to serve this country well. Give me guidance in making the difficult decisions that are necessary for this nation's welfare. Help the congress to work with me for the betterment of our citizens so that we may accomplish the major tasks put before us. Let the world live in peace and harmony in the years ahead and guide this country and my leadership for the betterment of all mankind."

The entire assembly of Senators, Representatives, cabinet members and galleryites stood up, and gave Kelli a tremendous ovation as she stepped down from the podium. During her State of the Union talk, she had nineteen major interruptions and pauses for applause. It was the largest recorded in the Republic's history. Most were for her comments about public education and health care. The media felt that these comments were excellent, and could be productive for progress.

There was an occasional interruption during her recommendations for term limits. The gray-heads in the Senate and the House of Representatives were not happy, and the media knew that they would not support this issue. Their seniority let them control the major committees in congress. "It's unconstitutional!", they remarked, and they would not support an amendment to the constitution that would limit their power.

Americans had gotten fed up with the previous do-nothing Congress, so they elected a new majority of Democrats to the House. The Senate Republicans still had a small majority and Preston Adams was back as the Majority Leader.

In some ways, the American public was becoming revolutionary in character and very demanding of their elected representatives. The laws of the land and, in particular, the Constitution, were being challenged more aggressively. It was felt that the Constitution, as time went by, had to be changed to adapt to a constantly growing diverse society. Democracy had taken hold around the world because everyone knew what was going on in everyone else's backyard and the media could easily portray it on television or through computers or other methods of communication. The time span for communication was infinitesimal, and everything was global now.

The United States was still the world leader in new scientific discoveries and innovative methods. The political ramifications of some of the recent advances in science and, in particularly, medicine were overwhelming. In the past, it had taken years of study to evaluate symptoms and accumulate data in order to diagnose some of the disease patterns to treat them properly. Genetic research was phenomenal in its application to medicine, and the environment still played a big role in your survival on earth. With the development of sophisticated imaging instrumentation with use of computers, CAT scans, magnetic resonance, ultrasound machines and computerized chemical testing, the long time span for discovering something new was shortened tremendously. Some of these new instruments could actually invade the brain and measure the various electrical potentials used in the thought process. This was mind-boggling. The use of embryo's eggs and stem cells to grow reparative tissue was finally working out and was helping to improve the quality of life, and extend the life span.

The globalization of economics because of worldwide competition had a marked effect on labor -- both east and west. The differential in the pay scale of the workers and the top executives had widened tremendously and was the main topic of discussion by the populace. The rich were getting richer and the poor were getting poorer. The middle class was disappearing. It was creating a lot of unrest, similar to the 'Decline and fall of the Roman Empire.' Labor in the Far East, particularly China, was so cheap that labor in the U.S.A. was being shut out of the market.

What was also disturbing was the increasing number of people on the steps of the Supreme Court building with placards, protesting or trying to influence the decisions of the Supreme Court Justices.

The people in the street felt that too many laws were being broken and that the Supreme Court had become too political. Their interpretation of the law had been inconsistent, and some felt, prejudicial. The court had issued fewer rulings then it usually puts out.

The Supreme Court had aged quite a bit during the past ten years with the older members in their seventies and eighties refusing to step down. They intended to sit on the bench for life. The longer they served the greater effect they had on the laws of the land. Some were also on an ego trip to expand their exposure in the history books and consolidate their legacies. Others were there to maintain a balance in the court concerning controversial legal issues. The news media and the press were more vocal about their rulings. The largest clamor came from the public because of inaction on specific controversial subjects. Some felt the inaction was due to their inability to comprehend the relevancy of the law. Others expressed the opinion that the aging of the justices hindered proper intellectual evaluation of the laws that were being challenged.

Security also had to be increased for the Justices, because the public was openly aggressive. The court was being exposed to public outrage more often. Some jeered and threw tomatoes and other unpleasant items at their limousines when they came to court. The instigators were not always caught. There was also a lot of vocal opposition, vicious placards, and letters telling them to resign. When a rock was thrown hitting the windshield of one of the Supreme Court Justice's limos, that went too far. Unfortunately, it was the Chief Justice's limo and James Stewart, the Chief Justice was mad!

"This has got to stop!" he hollered. "The Constitution allows for freedom of speech and assembly, but when it may cause me bodily harm, something has to be done about it and promptly. Justice must prevail!"

The culprit who threw the rock was caught and put in jail, but the damage was done. The local Afro-American judge in D.C. gave the assailant a short sentence because the assailant was also a member of the Afro-American community. He didn't want to start an uprising in his own group... he needed their support because he was an elected judge. Unfortunately, the responsible individual became a martyr and a celebrity when he got out.

A month later, in the Washington Times on the editorial page, there was an article titled: "Is it time for a change on the U.S. Supreme Court bench? Are the American people getting a proper evaluation of the laws of the land."

The editorial pages of the major newspapers also suggested that some of the Justices should retire and be replaced. Many of the articles actually gave the age and named the weak or feeble Justices. Unfortunately, they were in office for life, as written in the Constitution, and there was nothing that could be done about it.

Kelli's presidency also came under fire because of the gridlock that was evident in the U.S. Supreme Court. She finally decided to mention it in her press conferences hoping to get some of the older members to step down. The following week she brought it up.

George Venard, journalist from the Washington Post asked an appropriate question.

"President Palmer, how do you plan to correct the log jam we have in the U.S. Supreme Court? Congress has passed numerous laws that have been appealed in the federal courts. Many of the decisions of the federal courts are political and may be unconstitutional. The court is not addressing the complicated legal problems concerning genetics, cyberspace, computers, theft of computer data, invasion of confidentiality, the take-over of some of our major corporations by foreign countries, and many other problems. The Supreme Court is in a parking lot doing nothing!"

Kelli replied, "I agree that the Supreme Court has problems. I wonder if the older judges understand some of these modern complicated issues. They don't seem to have a clear understanding of science that is relevant. I worry about their health, and their ability to write clear judgments."

Bill Jones of the New York Times spoke up. "I also wonder whether some of our Justices are able to interpret some of our recent laws passed by Congress in regards to healthcare or complicated medical problems, such as the use of embryological transplant material, the growing of new human tissue. When does life start? What about the right to die, assisted suicide, and the use of genetic testing that could eventually predict the length of life for a human? They don't know anything about the human genome and its applications to laws."

"You're right!" said Kelli. "I also wonder if we should have a law that requires the Supreme Court Judges to have a physical exam every six months. Unfortunately, we do not have an age limit for the justices."

"That'll never happen because they'll veto it!" replied Jones. "They'll declare it unconstitutional. They have the last word."

"That demonstrates a weakness in our system," replied Kelli. "They really don't have any peer review."

Kathy Nordstrom from the Chicago Sun Times raised her hand. "What about your own disability or the Vice President's?"

"The Congress has not addressed the 25th amendment that concerns that problem. There's ambiguity in that amendment, too! I'm glad the press has brought up these questions today. With the help of the media, I hope to find some way to correct some of these deficiencies."

With that statement the press conference ended.

While the Supreme Court was in session in April, it became stuck on the appeal of a law passed by Congress, on the controversy of the makeup of the jury system. It concerned race, color, and ethnic groups. The media blasted the court because of its indecision.

It was quite obvious that it was getting almost impossible to get a major criminal conviction, because you needed unanimous consent of twelve jurors.

The U.S. Constitution of 1787 guaranteed trial by jury in all criminal cases tried in the U.S.A. It was based on English Common Law that dated back to the 11th century during Henry II's reign.

The jury had to consist of twelve people. A judge was present to instruct the jury as to the law and evidence, and the verdict had to be unanimous.

There is a big difference in the selection of juries in England and the United States and how they work.

The juries are selected at random in England and the decision does not have to be unanimous. Their system works well, but in the U.S.A., clever lawyers prune out potential jurors who might render a judgment against their client. In the U.S.A., the jury must give a unanimous decision.

Many cases are being won, based on the makeup of the juries – Afro-American, White, Hispanic, Asian, etc. More and more juries are deciding cases on the basis of political beliefs, rather than the law. The public became aware of this and became agitated because of what was happening... criminals were going free. On the Supreme Court steps, individual racial groups were polarizing and more police had to be assigned to prevent violence. There was gridlock in the courts and some obvious criminals were literally getting away with murder. The public didn't like this and expressed their anger.

There was also the continuing problem that some justices were not in good health. In fact, some were in bad health and shouldn't be on the bench. One of the Supreme Court justices, Justice Irving Goldstein, had to be brought into court every day in a wheelchair. He had obvious Parkinson's, had recovered from a stroke, and there was a question as to whether he actually knew what was going on – more important was whether he could interpret the Constitution properly.

Justice Emma Mayberry did not appear in court regularly because she had a major cancer operation in New York, and things weren't going well. She was debating resigning... just what type of operation she had done, was kept from the media. It was evident that she had lost quite a bit of weight and there was a rumor that her cancer had spread to her liver. The reason she didn't resign was because the court was equally divided on major issues. A Republican President had appointed her to the court and her party didn't want her to resign, even though she had a serious illness. A Democratic President could replace her and tilt the court.

Finally, the day arrived for a vote of the Supreme Court justices concerning the physical makeup of the juries, but three of the justices didn't show up in the courtroom.

2

UNIVERSITY COMPOUND
MEETING OF THE ISLAMIC CHIEFS
PESHAWAR, PAKISTAN

Hussein Hasir Haddad called a meeting of his Islamic chiefs together in Peshawar, Pakistan.

"The time has come for Islam to get even with some of the western Democratic countries. The House of Islam is being embarrassed by their actions. The sophisticated weapons of the United States have fired missiles which have landed in Afghanistan. We look like a bunch of idiots and weaklings on the world stage, and must do something to reestablish our image! Some of our brothers have been in prison too long! All Muslims are brothers, and the time has come to contact our Muslims brothers in the U.S.A. We will see if they are true brothers!"

"Do you plan to contact that Montana militia man, Tom Whitehall?" asked Rashid.

"No. We will ask our Muslims in America to do that. Maybe we'll let the Montana militia do our dirty work. We'll contact Muhammad Khan in Chicago. He's the leader of the Midwestern section of Muslims. Give him that coin we cut in two. Tell Khan to contact Whitehall. That plan Whitehall suggested may be a way to free our imprisoned brothers. Rashid, take two men with you when you contact Muhammad Khan in Chicago. Watch out for bugging devices and possible C.I.A. intervention."

When Rashid, the Brigade Commander, got on a plane in Peshawar with his two henchmen and headed to Karachi and then on to Frankfort and New York City, C.I.A. spies in the area reported his movements to the main C.I.A. compound in McLean, Virginia. Two agents were assigned to keep him under surveillance once he entered the country. Rashid made no attempt to hide his identity, and was easily recognized by the agents.

At Kennedy Airport, two Islamic Muslims known to the C.I.A. in New York City picked him up and drove to the Bronx.

He obviously was making no attempts to hide his tracks, as he checked into a religious mosque and was greeted by a mufti before going into the mosque. This area of the Bronx had quite a few Muslims living nearby so it would be difficult to set up a close surveillance. The C.I.A. decided to add more agents to the area to keep a close eye on him. When Rashid didn't come out of the mosque for three days, the C.I.A. realized they had lost their man. He had disappeared into the environs of the big city.

Three months later, Rashid returned to that same mosque in the Bronx and two days later boarded a plane at Kennedy to return to Peshawar, Pakistan. The C.I.A. had completely lost him and didn't know where he had been during those previous three months.

Most of the Supreme Court justices lived around Washington, D.C., either in Virginia or Maryland. They all had limousines provided by the government, with armed chauffeurs who were trained Treasury Secret Service Agents. The limousines were constructed with fancy bulletproof shaded glass, heavy metal bomb-proof flooring, and special tires. The communication systems built into the limos were the state of the art. Court was usually not in session until 10:00 A.M., so the justices were driven in on the major highways to D.C., arriving at about 9:00 A.M. so they could briefly review what was on the docket for the day with their law clerks.

James Stewart, the Chief Justice of the Supreme Court, lived on a farm in Culpepper, Virginia. His Secret Service security chauffeur, Jack Boyd, usually picked him up at about 8:00 A.M.

Jack usually picked up the *Washington Post*, and the *New York Times*, prior to his arrival at the farm. Justice Stewart would usually read the papers or peruse the headlines as Jack drove on Route 29 to Route 66 into the Capitol city.

The chauffeur had a tendency to drive briskly on the highway, usually going faster than 70 mph, and had been picked up several times for speeding. When the State Police realized that the occupant of the limo was the Chief Justice, no ticket was issued and the chauffeur had a smile on his face. Suddenly, on Route 29, he saw flashing lights from police cruisers ahead of him. He slammed on the brakes and a short distance ahead of him saw a tractor-trailer lying on its side, completely blocking the highway.

It was obvious that a bad accident had just occurred and the highway was beginning to look like a parking lot. One of the Virginia State Policemen was trying to direct the traffic to a small side road detour.

"What's up Jack?" asked Chief Justice Stewart.

"Another tractor trailer accident," he replied. "It looks like we may have a slight delay. The weather's cloudy and it's foggy today."

"Well, the court can't start until I get there," he replied, as he continued reading his papers.

"It looks like the State Police are starting a detour around the accident site. We probably ought to take it," said Jack.

"It's better than just sitting here in this parking lot. It will take them forever to clean up the mess. Why don't you swing the limo over?"

"There's a state cop coming our way. I'll ask him. Officer, I have a VIP in the limo. Is it a long detour?"

"Not really. I'll have one of the other cops drive in front of you and lead the way. Follow his cruiser."

"Thanks!" replied Jack.

The road for the detour was a two-lane dirt farm road that was quite bumpy. There were barbed wire cattle fences on both sides. The police cruiser preceded the limo, followed by another car, another cruiser, and other cars taking the detour.

After driving for about five minutes, the state trooper stopped the limo, and told Jack he knew a short cut they could take, and the other cars would continue on their route.

"Anything to get back on tract to D.C.," he replied.

After driving for an additional ten minutes into the farm country, the road dipped into a valley. There was a large cattle barn a short distance away from the road. The cruiser stopped and the trooper got out and walked back to the limo. Just before he got to the driver's side of the limo, he pulled his .45 caliber revolver out and said, "Driver, step out of the limo and put your hands up. No shenanigans, or you're dead."

"There must by some mistake, Officer," said Jack. "That's the Chief Supreme Court Justice in the backseat of my limo."

"Yes, I know," he replied. "No fancy moves when you get out of the limo."

Jack opened the door and stepped out. He wore a holster pistol, but he was covered. If he made a move for his gun, he'd be dead.

"Turn around, and put both hands on the roof."

As Jack put his hands on the roof, he received a crushing blow to the back of his head knocking him unconscious.

The disguised state trooper had accomplices in the car behind the limo, and they pulled Chief Justice Stewart out of the backseat.

"You won't be able to get away with this!" Stewart hollered. "You'll all be going to prison."

Before he could say another word, plastic tape was placed over his mouth, and handcuffs were put on his wrists. His suit jacket was cut off, and his shirtsleeves pulled up exposing his bare arm. He was quickly injected with a narcotic medication, and within seconds he slumped to the ground.

"I hope you didn't give him an overdose," commented the disguised officer.

"No, but he'll sleep for a long time."

The back door of the large cattle barn opened, and a small transport Bell model helicopter was rolled out. The two police cruisers, and the black limo were driven into the barn. Gasoline was poured over the cars and on the hay, and two timing devices that would ignite, were set to go off a few hours after they left.

The Chief Justice, who was out cold, was put on a stretcher and into the helicopter. The doors to the barn were shut, and the helicopter took off into the cloudy sky. It was an ideal day for disappearing into the clouds, because the ceiling was less than 500 feet. There was no way other planes would be able to follow if they flew close to the ground.

Associate Supreme Court Justice Calvin Hughes lived in a beautiful Virginia home on the outskirts of Fredericksburg, about an hour from Washington, D.C. He was the oldest member of the Court at 85 years, and was an obstreperous, boisterous jurist who was a staunch conservative. His health was poor, and you could see that he had severe trouble with his bone structures because he walked with a slow gait with a hunched back appearance. He obviously had male osteoporosis, or some other debilitating arthritic disease that affected his back. He rarely gave an interview to the press, but when he did, he was often asked, "When are you going to retire?"

"I'll retire when I feel good and ready," he replied. Oliver Wendell Holmes worked on the court in his nineties. "If I feel that my mental capacities diminish, I'll think about quitting."

"You may not recognize that your mental capacities are diminishing," said the reporter.

"I can tell when my memory and cognitive capacity is slipping. It isn't slipping yet!"

"You haven't been consistent in your Court rulings recently," another one of the reporters stated. "You've always been a conservative and now you're a liberal."

"What's wrong with that?" he replied. "As you get older, you become more liberal in your thinking. You want to give things away and do more good for the poor. It's like people believing in God, and going to church. As you get older, more people go to church and hope and pray there is a God because death is inevitable. A Supreme Court Justice gets more liberal as he gets older."

"Shouldn't you make room for some younger Justice?" he was asked.

"Not unless you can show me someone who is smarter than I am and knows the law better than I do. There ain't too many like that. I don't see anyone on the horizon."

"How about your health?"

"What about my health? It's perfect – never felt better!"

The media had big doubts about that statement. He was known to have made recent visits to the Mayo Clinic and John Hopkins Hospital. He had severe arthritis because he obviously had difficulty walking. He used a cane and sometimes he was bought into the courtroom in a wheelchair. He was also known to doze on the bench, and had recently fired three of his law clerks. It wasn't the first time… he was a difficult person to work for. One of the fired law clerks gave an interview to the press, and said that his mind was gone, and he should resign from the court.

The Washington and New York newspapers interviewed the law clerk, Sara Peterson, a Duke Law School graduate.

"Why were you fired by Justice Hughes?" she was asked.

"Because I argued about his opinions which he wasn't writing."

"What do you mean?"

"He'd ask all the law clerks to write up our own opinions about a case, then he'd select one to be given to the court."

"Isn't that what you were suppose to do?"

"Not really. There was no input by him. He made no revisions or constructive criticisms."

"How do you know this?" asked a New York reporter.

"Because John Pierce, a friend of mine and another of Judge Hughes' law clerks, submitted an opinion to Judge Hughes. He told Judge Hughes that he didn't understand the law pertaining to the case. Judge Hughes said, 'Don't worry about that.' That clerk's opinion was used by Justice Hughes without any changes."

"What you are saying is that the law clerks are writing his opinions, and he's just a figure head on that bench."

"That's right."

"As a Supreme Court law clerk, you are pledged to secrecy. If we publish your comments, it could hurt your career."

"I realize that. Somebody has to blow the whistle even if it involves a Supreme Court Justice. I'm not sure I want to practice law, anyway. I don't like the Socratic method of teaching law."

The next day, the entire interview of Sara Peterson was published in the Washington and New York papers. Justice Hughes was asked to comment about her remarks.

"Young law clerks are hired to assist the Supreme Court Justices in the interpretation of constitutional law. They are young lawyers in the learning mode and should be grateful for the experience that they are gaining working in my office. I fired Sara Peterson because she was an individualist who varied from the norm, and was not interpreting the law the way I wanted her to."

"Isn't her job to challenge your opinions?"

"Not really. She was too arrogant and did not compromise."

Every day Justice Hughes' limo arrived outside his home at 7:30 A.M.

He noted that there was a new driver in the front seat and commented about it as he stepped into the back seat.

"What happened to Bill Carpenter?' he asked.

"Bill has a dental appointment, and is having a root canal done today."

"Better him than me," said the Justice. "Did you pick up the newspapers?"

"Yes... they're over in the corner in the backseat... the *Washington Post,* the *New York Times and the Philadelphia Inquirer.*"

Justice Hughes took the papers and settled into the backseat, reading the papers as the limo pulled away from the driveway and eventually turned onto Route 95 heading for Washington.

After driving for about fifteen minutes, the driver made an abrupt turn onto an exit ramp around an overpass and headed in the opposite direction on Route 95. Justice Hughes was engrossed in his newspapers and didn't notice the change in direction. Thirty minutes later, the driver pulled off Route 95 at Exit 606, and then drove onto an uninhabited road. There was a large trailer truck parked on the side of the road with the back door opened. On the back of the truck there was a conveniently placed ramp leading into the big truck. The limo drove right up the ramp into the truck and the back door was quickly shut.

Justice Hughes didn't notice what had happened until he couldn't read the papers in the darkness.

"What the hell's going on here? What's happening?" he shouted. "I can't see my newspapers!"

Two men inside the back of the truck opened the back door of the limo, and jumped inside with the Justice. Because of his age and size, Justice Hughes was easy to subdue. He was quickly handcuffed and his mouth was taped shut. The truck quickly headed south on route 95.

Supreme Court Justice Monroe Fineberg lived in an attractive brownstone building in the wealthy old section of Georgetown. He was a 74-year-old bachelor and former Dean of the Yale Law School. He had served on the Supreme Court for fifteen years, and was a prolific writer for the Law Review Journal. He was also active in the various arts programs around Washington, D.C., serving on the board of the John F. Kennedy Art Center, and the Smithsonian Institute. He was frequently seen at the symphony or White House special events.

Justice Fineberg was a robust individual, an immaculate dresser, who wore expensive British or Italian suits, and custom made shirts and bow ties. He had been a bachelor all of his life, and when asked about it, replied that he didn't have time for women.

He believed in maintaining a rigid constitutional interpretation of the law. As a result, he was often the target of liberal groups, such as the American Civil Liberties Union. He was not one to back off on a fight about legal matters, and was often thought to be too free in expressing his opinions in public to the news, and television media.

Because of his openness to the press, his limo was often the target of protesters when he arrived at the Court. It had been pelted with tomatoes and eggs on more than one occasion, until they blocked off the posterior entrance to the Supreme Court building.

Justice Fineberg had had a severe heart attack in the past, with coronary bypass surgery, and, because of that, was a health fitness nut... working out daily at the Congress Health Fitness Center. He usually arrived early in the morning before court went into session.

Every day he was picked up by his limo at 6:30 A.M., and taken to the Congress Fitness Center where he worked out for about an hour, and then had a light breakfast before the court session started.

One day, he had severe chest pain while the court was in session, and had to leave the bench. A doctor was called; he was examined, and taken to the George Washington University Hospital ER for evaluation. His electrocardiogram showed some new changes and he was admitted to the hospital. His cardiologist was called and an extensive cardiac work-up was done. This revealed some fluid in his lungs. A special scan was done of the heart, and it showed old muscle damage and a dilated enlarged heart. He was given antibiotics, diuretics, cardiac drugs, and had to remain in the hospital for two weeks. The Washington papers speculated that he might retire because of his recent hospitalization.

When Justice Fineberg saw the articles, he called the news-papers and blasted them. He stated, "There's no way that I will leave the Court unless I drop dead." He blamed the press as the culprits, causing him all that bad publicity. He also called the senior newspaper editors on the phone, and told them that they were all stupid and misinformed. He wrote a letter to the publisher and told him to get some new editors.

"I will be returning to the bench in one week," he vehe-mently declared.

When his week was up, he returned to the Court in a wheel-chair. It was obvious that he had not fully recovered from his recent illness. He looked pale and ashen and was still chronically ill with congestive heart failure. He coughed continually with wheezing and was a deep concern to his fellow Supreme Court Justices. They were worried that he might have a catastrophe in front of the court and drop dead. Many of his friends advised him to quit... not Jus-tice Fineberg. His anger and paranoia persisted. He felt that every-one was out to get him.

"I'm more important than the President," he said. "He can be thrown out by the Congress or the electorate. I'm a judge for life!"

The second day after coming back from the hospital, he had another severe coughing spell in court. The other Supreme Court

Justices watched him intently. They had difficulty concentrating on the case being presented before them. The Chief Justice noticed this and called for a recess. In his chambers, he discussed the problem with Justice Fineberg. Fineberg was adamant. He told Chief Justice Stewart, "There's no way I'm going to quit, and let some young immature pompous ass try to solve this country's difficult legal problems."

"You're having trouble breathing, Monroe. How can you function?" asked the Chief Justice.

"My mind is as good as anyone's," he replied. "In a short period of time the coughing spells will go away."

The next afternoon he went into another coughing spasm, and got blue in the face. He popped some pills into his mouth, and pulled out a medical inhaler from his pocket.

The entire courtroom became silent and all the justices watched apprehensively as he huffed and puffed alternately using his inhaler, trying to break up the bronchial spasm with the loud barking cough. His breathing finally returned to normal after using the inhaler for approximately five minutes. He still was short of breath as he blurted out, "I'm doing fine. Continue the presentation of the case."

The lawyer presenting the case was disturbed because the justices were more interested in watching how their fellow jurist was doing with his coughing spasm, and were not listening to his presentation.

"Your Honor, do you want me to repeat the case?"

Before the Chief Justice could reply, Justice Fineberg hollered out, "Of course not! I heard every single word."

Chief Justice Stewart, and the other justices were embarrassed. He banged his gavel down.

"Court will be recessed again until tomorrow. Monroe, I'd like to see you in my chambers."

"I'll be there," replied the Justice.

"Monroe, you're too sick to be sitting on the bench. You sound like you ought to be in the hospital."

"I have a chronic cough from the irritation of the fluid in my lungs. I've been given a diuretic to get rid of all that fluid. My heart specialist has assured me that my mind is perfect, and the cough should go away."

"You're disrupting the court with all you're coughing. I hate to say it, but it's an embarrassment to the court."

"I'm sorry about that... however, I don't plan to step down, or resign. Why don't you recess the court for a few days so I can recover."

"I'll recess the court for two days, if you promise to see your cardiologist, and get some pills to stop your coughing."

"I'll do that," he replied.

Court resumed after two days, Monroe's coughing persisted, and because he wouldn't quit, the Court arranged for a paramedic and hospital stat-cart to stay on standby out of sight in the back of the courtroom. To compound Justice Fineberg's problems, when he tried to return to the Congress fitness center to work out, he promptly passed out on the floor, and had to be resuscitated with oxygen. It hit the nightly newspapers, and prime time T.V. Photos showed him lying on the ground receiving treatment. It was obvious that he was becoming an embarrassment to the other Justices, and they didn't know what to do. There was nothing in the Constitution that described how a Supreme Court Justice could be replaced if he was disabled. There was no way they could keep him out of the courtroom. He was a member of the Court for life.

Justice Fineberg's illness became a prime topic in the media. They wanted to ask him numerous questions about his health... he gave no interviews, and told his law clerks, and secretarial help to keep their mouths shut if they valued their jobs. He had a run-in with his cardiologist who advised him to quit because his heart muscle was giving out and medications weren't working... there wasn't a lot that they could do about it except for a possible heart transplant. He was told that he was too old for a heart transplant, and wasn't a good candidate because he had chronic kidney disease and a poor liver.

Two weeks after the passing out episode, parked in the front of his house, in his front driveway, instead of a limo, was a funeral hearse. The neighbors figured that he had finally died... morticians carried a body out of the house on a stretcher and drove away.

3

SUPREME COURT CALAMITY

When the three Supreme Court Justices didn't show up for Court, the Court session was canceled. It was not immediately realized what had happened.

It was not unusual when one justice did not show up for Court. All they needed was a quorum of six justices to function. It was most unusual when the Chief Justice and two other associated justices did not show up or did not notify the Court of their absence.

However, it took awhile to learn what had taken place. When the security agents did not check in, and a search was made for their whereabouts, it eventually became evident that three Supreme Court Justices were missing and nobody knew where they were. It didn't take long to realize that they had probably been kidnapped. The F.B.I., C.I.A and the Armed Forces were notified, and a nationwide search for their whereabouts began.

The three abductions were perfectly coordinated. It was a quick smooth professional job. The limousines and police cars eventually were found, and were burned to a crisp along with the barn near Culpepper. There were no clues that could be identified. They eventually found out about the hearse, which had been stolen the night before. It too was missing. The Virginia State Troopers, and the Secret Service chauffeurs were all missing and presumed dead.

The President was notified about the kidnappings, and security was increased around the White House, the Capitol and all Federal buildings. Kelli went on television to announce what had happened.

"My fellow Americans, something terribly tragic has happened. Three Supreme Court Justices are missing and presumed to be kidnapped. Terrorists have struck right at the heart of our Justice System. We are offering a five million dollar reward to anyone who assists in the safe return of our Justices. If the Justices are harmed in any way, the reprisal will be swift for the individuals involved, and will include the country of origin of the terrorists. The United States cannot and will not tolerate what has happened."

SITUATION ROOM
WHITE HOUSE
WASHINGTON, D.C.

The National Security Council, the Joint Chiefs of Staff, senior members of the Senate and House, and the Secretary of the Treasury were called to an emergency meeting.

The disruption of the U.S. Supreme Court by the kidnapping of the three Justices would have a serious effect on the daily function of the government. It also had a profound effect on the morale of the people. The men and women in the street were visibly disturbed. How could this happen? As each hour went by without finding the Justices, the apprehension increased. What had gone wrong?… three justices missing during the same time period.

The people became outwardly disturbed. Mobs gathered and picketed outside the Supreme Court building in D.C. and the other Federal Court buildings around the country. Some carried placards that were outright antagonistic and hostile: "good riddance for three bums", "Appoint honest new Judges", "Keep politics out of the courtroom", "We need brains not politicians in the courtroom."

President Palmer, wanted some questions answered immediately. She directed her first question to the Secretary of the Treasury, since his department is in charge of providing Secret Service protection to the Supreme Court Justices.

"Secretary Hart, what happened? How could the people who did this dastardly act get away without leaving a trail? Three kidnappings! Supreme Court Justices gone! I can't believe it!"

"Ms. President, this looks like a well-planned terrorist plot with kidnappers working as well rehearsed professionals. I agree with you. No shots were fired, and the chauffeur security agents are all missing and probably dead. We suspect that they may have used a helicopter to kidnap the Chief Justice, one was seen flying low in the area, but we're sure that's not the method used in the other abductions."

"We ought to be able to find a helicopter," replied Kelli. "They're not easy to hide."

"I agree," said Hart. "The trouble is that we've had too many people calling in and telling us they heard airplanes flying low in their local vicinity. Our whole Army would have to be out searching."

"If it's necessary to call out the Army to look for those terrorists, I'll do it! Should we do that, General Montgomery?"... Montgomery was the Chairman of the Joint Chiefs.

"It might be too obvious to the kidnappers," he replied. "I'm certainly willing to consider it if we have some clues about where to begin looking."

"That's the problem," said F.B.I. Chief, George Parton. "Nobody saw the kidnappers. They probably wore human face-masks that looked very authentic, and skin-colored rubber gloves. They destroyed any evidence that was in the limousines and police cruisers. The cars were burned to a crisp and their license plates are missing. What's most disturbing is that the Chief Justice's Secret Service chauffeur didn't check in with the Security Center when he was stopped at the truck accident site. The state trooper who remained at the accident site was not involved with the kidnappings. One of the state troopers was probably paid off to cooperate with the kidnappers. The chauffeur obviously was not concerned about the Chief Justice's safety at that time. This gave one group of kidnappers a head start, when they diverted his limo into that big barn in Culpepper."

"Do we have any clues at all? Why would he check in because a truck had an accident on Highway 29 causing a delay in his limo?" asked Kelli.

"That's probably why he didn't check in."

"Have we heard from anyone?'

"None."

"Have they tried to contact anyone?'

"No."

What are we doing to find these people?"

"We're trying to find out where there might be a helicopter or a hearse missing. Our crime lab is trying to come up with something out of those burned vehicles. We're also questioning the owner of that farm where the Chief Justice was abducted. He denies everything. He said he was in the barn a week before and everything looked normal. It was used for hay storage, and milking. He sold all his cows a year ago with the milking equipment and it was recently renovated. He's mad, and he wants the government to pay for that barn that burned down."

"If they used a helicopter, how did they get a helicopter into a cow barn without anyone seeing it?"

"It probably happened at night in that remote farm country. It could have been flown in from another site, or was brought in by a big truck, and the propellers put back on. Who knows how they did it?"

"We don't look very good on the world stage if we allow our Supreme Court Justices to be kidnapped," said Kelli. "Anyone have any brilliant suggestions?"

There was a strange silence around the room.

Kelli was frustrated and upset. She finally said something she might regret. "Gentlemen, if we don't catch these criminals, and if any of those Supreme Court Justices are harmed, I'm afraid I'm going to have to make recommendations for some big changes in my Administrative Staff and Department Chiefs, including the Secret Service, and the Joint Chiefs. We just can't have this happen in this country!"

After making that statement, Kelli got up, and walked out of the room.

Nothing happened for a week. The stress was unbearable. The Justices had disappeared off the face of the earth.

The F.B.I. and the Armed Forces were frantically looking for a helicopter that was missing from an Army reserve storage area in Texas. It was nowhere to be found. Helicopters can practically land on a dime, so it could be anywhere within five hundred miles of the site of the abductions. They located the funeral home that was missing a hearse in Washington, D.C. It had been reported. There were no clues as to who might have stolen it.

The Supreme Court had to close down, and the rest of the Court members went underground in seclusion.

One week later, a ransom note was received at the White House. It briefly stated; "Release all Islamic prisoners, who were involved in the World Trade Center bombing, the Saudi Arabia bombing, the Egyptian and Kenya bombing, and the bombing in Chicago and Seattle... you have one week." Photographs of the judges who looked tired and haggard were with the note.

There were two terrorists over eighty years of age that were involved with the Trade Center bombing, in New York's penitentiary and six others in mid-western prisons.

The F.B.I and C.I.A. met with President Palmer. They had found out nothing.

"What should I do?" she asked.

The F.B.I. director spoke up, "I've given a lot of thought about what has happened. In some way, we have to get the kidnappers to give us some kind of a clue."

"Perhaps you should announce on T.V. and in the papers that you need to have proof that they're still alive. Once that happens, say that you'll release the prisoners.

"That's giving in to their demands."

"Not really, until you release the prisoners."

"We're desperate. I'm willing to try."

That evening, Kelli went on T.V. at 6:30 P.M., and then 10:00 P.M. She requested evidence that the Supreme Court Justices were still alive.

At midnight, a phone call was made to the White House from somewhere in Pennsylvania.

"You'll receive a video with the Justices' pictures and voices in 72 hours. Once you receive that, you have 48 hours to release the prisoners, or they're dead! The three Supreme Court Justices are hidden in three separate areas. If you find any one of the Justices, the other two will be killed immediately. I suggest you call the blood hounds off."

The video arrived the next day and was immediately worked over by the C.I.A. and the F.B.I. Copies were made and the Armed Services got involved. Spy satellites were used to comb the area 750 miles around Washington and Virginia. One frame on the video showed a large cattle barn in the distance. Using the global digital satellite system, they were able to figure out the general area, and later a more specific area in Rocky Mount, North Carolina. They finally located the suspected area by enlarging the frame, and using surveyor's methods and the 3-D satellite mapping. SWAT teams surrounded the area and waited, keeping it under tight surveillance. They didn't want the other two Justices killed if there was only one there.

The government kept its word, and released the Islamic Alliance prisoners, putting the releases on national television. However, the F.B.I. kept a close eye on them.

The next night, around midnight, a black Town Car pulled up to the barn in High Point, North Carolina, and six people came out to get in the car. Three were obviously handcuffed and their mouths were taped. Telescopic night lenses, and sophisticated night vision apparatus recorded the event. The kidnappers had lied. All the Justices were in one place. Just as they got ready to get into the car, SWAT teams converged on them with bright spotlights and guns. One shot was fired, and one of the Justices fell to the ground. The Chief Justice had been hit in the leg by a gun fired by a SWAT team member. One of the abductors was shot, and killed as he fled. The others raised their arms in surrender.

The Muslim prisoners, who had been released, were picked up, and the abductors of the Justices were questioned. The military took them into custody. In a very short period of time, they admitted the whole plot. Those Marines certainly have a way of doing their job! Tom Whitehall's militia, and the Islamic Alliance in Peshawar were the culprits.

Kelli went on T.V. the next day with the F.B.I., C.I.A. and the Armed Forces. The whole story was told… but not completely. Some dramatic changes were taking place.

Two of the older Supreme Court Justices decided their places on the bench would be vacated immediately. The job was too hazardous. Chief Justice Stewart also resigned after recovering from his leg wound. One of the Justices, Justice Fineberg, who had been kidnapped, almost died from a cardiac arrhythmia, and had to be hospitalized for eight weeks. He was a basket case and resigned later. Justice Hughes resigned also. Five Supreme Court Justices in all resigned from the Court. President Kelli Palmer now had an enviable opportunity that no other President had. She would be able to appoint five new Supreme Court Justices. The Republicans were in an uproar even though they still had a majority in the Senate and had to advise and consent.

4

ADVISE AND CONSENT

The Constitution did not provide for the sudden resignations of five Supreme Court Justices. They were appointed for life and usually the resignations came one at a time; over a long time frame or due to a fatal illness. There was nothing in the history books to use for guidelines in coping with this development. The appointment process was usually extremely difficult... the President would recommend an individual and then the Senate Judicial Committee would probe for weaknesses in the candidates' credentials... all sorts of controversy would develop. It usually took forever to get the Senate to approve one candidate, let alone five. The challenge presented was formidable... every ethnic group wanted a member to sit on the Supreme Court and the gender make-up would also have to be addressed.

The public definitely wanted to play a role in the selection process. Large groups with placards continued to assemble in front of the Supreme Court buildings and picketed the Capitol grounds.

The number of picketing Americans increased daily and additional police had to be assigned to control the mob. The Senators on the Judicial Committee were aware of what was transpiring because it was on TV and in the news media... the public wanted quick action... that wasn't possible. The candidates had to be scrutinized by the F.B.I. and their past records had to pass the litmus test.

The President was also aware of what was happening and she realized that she needed the cooperation of both parties to accomplish anything. She decided to have a personal meeting with the Republican Senate Majority Leader, Preston Adams.

WHITE HOUSE MEETING

"Preston, it's nice of you to come."

"Thank you, Ms. President. I realize we both have a Constitutional problem."

"It's about the Supreme Court appointments, isn't it?"

"Yes. I consider it a bipartisan challenge."

"You're sitting in the catbird seat."

"Not really. The public is demanding immediate action and we both know that's impossible... we could have a riot on our hands."

"I know. We can't be too hasty, however. Those men and women that we appoint to the court will have a greater influence on this country than you or I... they're appointed for life and we're elected."

"That's a weakness in our system," declared Kelli. "There's nothing in the Constitution to get rid of incompetent or sick justices."

"You'll never get an amendment through Congress to change the system," said Preston. "The lawyers sitting on that court have the final word."

"I'm not a lawyer," replied Kelli. "I don't believe our founding fathers meant it to be that way."

"You may be right, Kelli! How do you plan to go about expediting the selection process?"

"That's where you come in," she replied.

"If it's for the good of the country, I'll help! If it's for the good of your party, you have a problem!"

"That's fair enough," replied Kelli.

"Keep talking," said Preston. "I'm listening."

"First and foremost, I want to maintain diversity on the Supreme Court. I do not want any ethnic group to dominate the court. I want to appoint two women and three men... at least one Hispanic, one Afro-American, one Asian and two others."

"Does your diversity also apply to their thinking process or political learnings?"

"I think that politics should be left out of the court," replied Kelli. "The judges can have differences in political philosophies but should not be straight line party participants."

"That will never happen. The judges that get appointed when one party is in control usually votes and thinks like that party. Do you plan to appoint conservatives or liberals?"

"I would like to appoint individualists that are free thinkers – not classified as one or the other. I want the judges to place America foremost in their minds."

"My! You certainly have ambitious plans, Ms. President. How do you propose to find people like that?"

"That's why I'm asking for your help."

"I'll try to help," replied Preston.

"I've asked the American Bar Association, the Trial Lawyers Group and the Deans' of the law schools to submit names for consideration."

"I'd like to see that list when you get it. Maybe we'll be able to agree on some candidates."

"Good... I should have it within a week. I'll have a courier bring it to your office."

Before breaking up, they both agreed not to release any information about their meeting to the press.

The Republicans were in an uproar even though they still had a majority in the Senate and eventually would have to Advise and Consent. There were continuing accusations that President Palmer was trying to pack the Supreme Court... the *Washington Press Corps* was screaming for a press conference... they wanted to question the President. Both Preston and Kelli continued to keep quiet. Kelli finally sent a list of names that she had received to Preston. A few days later, she decided to call him.

"Have you gone over the list that I sent you? Have you got any prospective candidates?" she asked.

"Yes," he replied.

"Why don't you come over for dinner at the White House tonight. We'll compare lists."

"I'll be there at 6:00 P.M."

Kelli and Preston exchanged lists after dinner. About one-third of the names for consideration were duplicates. They both looked at each other in amazement and smiled.

"I see that we are not too far apart on some of the candidates," she said.

"I am as surprised as you are, Kelli."

"Why don't we start by discussing the justices that we both agree on. We'll number them one through five."

"We might be burning the midnight oil."

"I'm game if you are."

They started out by selecting one Hispanic and one Afro-American but got hung up on the Asian candidate. There weren't many Asian justices in the American Appellate Court System. They found a couple out in Hawaii and selected one of them. Finally, around midnight they completed a list of ten names. They were numbered one through ten. Kelli brought out some champagne and they clinked glasses.

"Preston, I'm going to give a press conference tomorrow and release this list of candidates to the media. Will you stand next to me on the podium? I want the public to know that we worked together. I suspect that we're both going to have lots of questions. Some people won't like what we've done."

"What time is the press meeting?"

"Ten o'clock in the morning."

"I'll have to think about it overnight," he replied. "I'm not sure that I want to take the heat."

WHITE HOUSE PRESS CONFERENCE

At 10:00 A.M., Kelli went to the pressroom. She noted that Senator Preston Adams was sitting in the front row.

"Members of the White House Press, I have some good news! I know that you've been waiting to receive a list of names that I recommend for consideration to be on the Supreme Court. It will be given to you shortly. Sitting in the audience is our Senate Majority Leader, Preston Adams. I would like him to join me up here at the podium. He has been instrumental in helping me make

up this list... It has been a long arduous task. Without his support, I could never envision a selection of properly qualified candidates."

Preston got up, walked to the podium and stood next to Kelli.

"Preston and I, both agreed that we should try to maintain diversity in the Supreme Court in regards to ethnicity and gender and to select for consideration, candidates that are basically centrists in their thinking, but individualists that will place the needs of their country before politics. We hope to maintain a balance in the court with judges that will adjudicate the laws that will benefit our people for many years to come. We both hope that the Senate Judicial Committee will interview the candidates that we have selected and expedite the process so that our government can get back to normal.

I wish to again personally thank Senator Adams for continuing to demonstrate his bipartisan leadership qualities in the Senate. He has shown that being an American is more important than being a Republican or a Democrat."

Suddenly without prompting, the Washington Press Corps stood up and there was prolonged applause.

When they sat down, Kelli announced:

"We'll take your questions now."

Marilyn Osborn, the head of the Washington Press Corps got up and was recognized by Kelli.

"I'd like to direct my question at Senator Adams. Senator, did you clear this list of names with the members of your own party on the Judicial Committee?"

"Yes, with the key senior members. After going over the list with President Palmer... it took us until midnight last night. I called the senior members of my Party and arranged to have an early breakfast with them. They agreed with my choices. There are both Republican and Democratic appointed Appellate Court Justices on that list. Also, there is a Professor of Law from Columbia University Law School, who has no Party affiliation."

There was a silence in the audience that followed his answer. He obviously had taken the wind out of Osborn's sails. She was trying to create controversy and Preston would have none of it.

Bill Kern from the *Chicago Sun Times* was called on next. "Senator Adams, how long do you think it will take the Senate to finish the hearings for the Supreme Court candidates?"

"Hopefully, it will take six weeks to three months. If we don't get our judicial system back on track promptly, we will all suffer."

"How do you plan to accomplish this?" asked Sara Reston of *the New York Times.*

"I plan to meet with the members of the Judicial Committee and tell them that the selection of the five new justices is a subject that our party should not drag out for political gain."

That statement was like a bombshell when the press digested it's meaning... the journalists in the pressroom became silent... then there was a hum of discussion amongst them. The Washington Press realized that the Senate Majority Leader was backing President Kelli Palmer and that the impending controversy about the selection of the jurists might be short lived.

Jack Johnson of the *St. Louis Post Dispatch* was recognized. "Senator, did you have any specific characteristics that you used in the selection of the names?"

"Yes. I wanted good, healthy, vibrant individuals to be chosen. I suggested that they all have a complete history and physical examination for perusal of the Judicial Committee. We can't have a bunch of sick jurists trying to comprehend difficult legal problems. We just went through that and it was a debacle."

Later that week, the Senate Majority Leader spoke to his colleagues on the Judicial Committee. There were some heated discussions that transpired. One of the senior senators felt that Preston was wrong to support Kelli. There would be much political gain by creating controversy. He was told that what he was doing might hurt the Republican Party. Preston didn't buy it and asked for a confidence vote. He got it and that was the end of the opposition... the Senators weren't stupid. They knew that they had to deal with Preston to get their pet bills on the docket. They also knew that the public was backing Kelli and if they wanted to get reelected, they needed a good press.

It took three months for the five Supreme Court Justices to be confirmed by the Senate. Preston received accolades from the media for his constructive attitude in solving the Supreme Court vacancies. He appeared on numerous TV news programs and talk shows and his prestige increased immensely. The Republican Party benefited also. It knocked the opposition within his party for a loop.

5

SECOND CONSTITUTIONAL CONVENTION

Kelli was quickly back in good graces with the public, so six months later, she decided to try to make the changes in the Constitution she wanted while the iron was hot. Something drastic had to be done to get the country back on the right track… it's global image had been tarnished.

She decided to go on a countrywide tour to all the state legislators to lobby for a Constitutional Convention for proposing amendments. The abduction of the Supreme Court Justices had focused on the importance of the Court. Kelli scheduled press conferences about the Constitutional convention, and got excellent television coverage. The recent Supreme Court resignations had left a big void in the justice system of the U.S.A. and there was nothing in the Constitution to prevent it from happening again. The court needed intelligent, healthy justices on the bench and the make-up of the new court was now changed – aged, disabled Justices could not be tolerated. There had to be an age limit and disability clause for removal. The media agreed with Kelli, and felt that the time had come to make the changes.

Kelli also wanted amendments for term limits and campaign finance reform. Not all the members of Congress agreed. Most of its senior members controlled the key committees. The chairmanships gave them prestige and political power in all branches of government and they controlled the money. Kelli's plan could upset their applecart. The senior Senators were outspoken in their opposition and felt that she would be unsuccessful in her undertaking. They also objected to the amount of favorable publicity that she was getting. Big corporations controlled the media and they objected to Kelli's plans and openly opposed it.

A prominent senior TV journalist, Bill Jones, got involved and was very outspoken in supporting Kelli. Kelli was upset when that same prominent journalist, who had supported her campaign was shot and killed. The F.B.I. got involved but couldn't find out who the assassin was.

In addition, a barrage of crank letters and threats to the President's life were sent to the White House. More security agents had to be assigned to protect Kelli when she went to the State Legislators.

After six months, Kelli got the endorsement of over fifty percent of the states to support a second Constitutional Convention. Three key states that she had to get were Texas, Florida and Illinois. It was getting harder to do as she approached the two-thirds number that were necessary to succeed. She finally got Florida, when Hispanics, Cubans and Afro-Americans, united to picket the Florida State Capitol in Tallahassee.

Kelli wanted to get Texas because that state was one of the most vocal in opposition to her plans. The two senators from the state and the governor got into the fight and got some oil corporations to give them "big bucks" to finance TV ads opposed to her drive. She also received two letters from Texas, which the F.B.I. looked at... threatening her life.

The F.B.I. chief advised Kelli not to make the trip. When she insisted on going, he beefed up the number of secret service agents and sent one of his senior assistants down to Austin, Texas, to look the situation over.

When the F.B.I. agent got back, he told his chief that the capitol building where the legislature met in Texas, had lots of nooks and crannies and would be difficult to secure.

"Your job is to protect the President," replied the chief. "Alert the local police and do whatever you have to do so she's not harmed. Someone tried to shoot Kelli when she was the Vice President. They almost got her that time in California... maybe she'll listen this time."

When Kelli was approached about going to Texas, she said, "No one's stopping me! I knew there would be opposition, but sometimes you have to assume a personal risk to reach your goal. I'll take that risk!"

The F.B.I. chief was not happy. He was aware of President John Kennedy's assassination in Dallas... and he was not about to have another assassination in that state, particularly on his watch. He decided to personally check out the set-up. He flew to Austin, Texas and met with the police chief.

"We'll need metal detectors installed at all the entrances and exits where the President is going to speak. I'd also like you to beef up the state police. We won't announce the route that the motorcade will take coming to the state capitol. I'll fly down some special equipment and a Plexiglas bulletproof glass shield for the podium."

Kelli took Air Force One to Austin, Texas. A C-135 freight plane proceeded her flight with the bulletproof limousine and other equipment that they used whenever she traveled. Six hundred security people were involved with her visit.

When the plane landed at the Austin, Texas airport, she got into her limo... which was proceeded by Texas State Police on motorcycles and surrounded by six special sport vehicles that were filled with armed Secret Service Agents. The motorcade traveled from the airport and arrived at the Texas State Capitol where there were pickets, carrying placards opposing her visit. Printed on the placards were: "Leave The Constitution Alone", "Don't Fool With The Supreme Court", "Get Women Out Of Politics"...not all the placards were against Kelli. Some college students carried signs that said: "Go for It Kelli," and another said, "Term Limits Are For Real", still another said "Campaign Financing Stinks". There seemed to be more in favor than against.

Kelli insisted in walking down the aisle to the podium instead of entering from the rear... four Secret Service Agents walked with her, surrounding her. All the people in the large chamber stood up.

She wore a dark blue suit, with a white blouse and a red kerchief tied around her neck. Her glistening red hair and brilliant green eyes and perfect white teeth were highlighted as her confident smile lit up the chambers. She looked Presidential, projecting her confidence to the Texas audience.

All the Texas State Legislators were present in the chambers to hear the President's pitch for a second Constitutional Convention. They were willing to listen but most were opposed... Texans did not support her on Election Day. She finally reached the podium. After much applause, the audience sat down. Kelli knew exactly what she wanted to say.

"Members of the Legislature of this great state of Texas"... that was all she had to say... all the people in the chamber stood up again and cheered. Finally, they stopped.

"This state has made history... at the Battle of the Alamo, fighting for independence... many brave Texans lost their lives, including Jim Bowie and Davey Crockett. You all know the battle cry, 'Remember the Alamo'? General Sam Houston whipped Mexican General Santa Anna in a bloody battle at San Jacinto. Once that was accomplished, the great state of Texas joined our nation in 1846... Members of this Texas legislature, we have another great fight on our hands. I'm trying to change the Constitution.

Congress in Washington has failed to act in proposing amendments to clean up the mess that we have. Politicians are literally buying public office with the support of corporations... that includes the office of the Presidency, the House of Representatives and the Senate. From the East Coast to the West Coast, state, local, and national races, are being corrupted by campaign finance contributions. We need campaign finance reform. Term limits are also necessary in order to get the incumbents that control the committees in Congress out of office. New fresh young politicians that are innovative will help us make laws that adapt to our changing society. Our Supreme Court Justices in Washington should have an age limit and method of removal for disability. The recent debacle that we just went through demonstrates that need. Our founding fathers recognized that changing circumstances and conditions might flaw the Constitution after it took effect; they therefore, determined not to continue the disastrous amending procedure of the articles of Confederation. They realized that Congress might not act, so they voted to permit Congress to call a convention to prepare amendments at the request of two-thirds of the states.

If two-thirds of the legislatures of the states call for a Constitutional Convention to propose amendments and those amendments are ratified by three-fourths of the states or by conventions in the three-fourths of the states, the new amendments are then valid for all Intents and Purposes as part of the Constitution... that's why I'm here to talk to you. We now have sixty percent of the states in favor, and if the great state of Texas agrees, we will go over the top and have enough votes to call for a second Constitutional Convention. I feel..."

Suddenly a member of the Texas legislature, sitting in the middle section of the second row, stood up and hollered,

"Texans will never support that! He quickly pulled a shiny object out of his vest and pointed it at Kelli... she recognized it... it was an automatic pistol.

He pulled the trigger and six shots were fired.

"Oh my God!" she exclaimed, as she fell to the ground behind the podium. Two Washington journalists sitting in the audience saw what happened... some of the bullets were tracer bullets that hit the plexiglass shield. They saw the President fall to the floor.

"Those shots were aimed right at the President."

"Was she hit?"

"She's down."

"Is the President dead?"

"Could be. It looks like she might be."

Complete bedlam ensued. Two of the Secret Service men on the podium standing near the plexiglass shield were shot. State police and Secret Service men got between the assassin and the President. A legislator sitting next to the assassin, attempted to grab the gun out of his hand, but was shot... blood erupted from his neck. Another Texan stood up behind the assassin and put his arms around his chest, pushing downward, stripping the gun out of his hand. The State Police and Secret Service Agents descended on the assassin and he was subdued and handcuffed. The legislator, who had been shot in the neck, slumped to his seat and a State Policeman quickly put pressure on the bullet entry site to control the bleeding.

Kelli was not hit. However, the Secret Service Agent resting his body over hers, was. There was blood all over his jacket. He was hit by a bullet in the shoulder, but was not critically wounded. Kelli was whisked out of the chamber by the Secret Service. Three people were shot by the assassin.

The Texas legislature put the issue of the second Constitutional Convention on the back burner. It was too controversial... the media and people in Texas did not agree. They had seen the assassination attempt and were horrified. They petitioned the state to have a referendum. Thousand of Texans marched in the streets. The state legislature got the message and took up the subject again and voted unanimously for the second Constitutional Convention.

Once Texas voted, the necessary two-thirds was in the ballot box. The states requested that the U.S. Congress convene a second Constitutional Convention for proposing amendments.

Philadelphia was again chosen as the site, and an agenda was set up for discussions of what was thought to be weaknesses in the original document.

SECOND CONSTITUTIONAL CONVENTION

The original Constitution was not all-inclusive, and wasn't meant to be. Parts of it had been placed on the shelf and a new Constitution, or at least important new amendments to it, were now to be discussed, and actually were struggling for change.

In the past, the Congress felt that the Supreme Court would rule against any change in the Constitution, and in particular changes that would limit their tenure. A Constitutional Convention could change that. The problem of "just who was in charge here," the states or the Federal government, was a perennial challenge for the court. Article 1, Section 8 gives Congress the power to impose taxes, regulate commerce, declare war, coin money, protect copyrights, etc., but does it have implied powers or just those expressly granted. Liberals feel that affirmative action should be continued, but is it violating the Constitutional guarantee of equal protection?

The Philadelphia convention convened with a tremendous amount of hoopla with worldwide attention on what was to be discussed. Very few of the Constitutional Convention members were congressional members. Actually, the big states tried to dominate the convention, but were unsuccessful, and rightfully so. The following amendments were decided on and passed.

1. PRESIDENTIAL ELECTION REFORM

Both major parties reconciled their differences about the Presidential election reform. There had to be a better way of voting for the President. There were too many variables and illegal ways of stuffing the ballot box. They agreed on the following changes:

The election day for the President is to be declared a mandatory holiday. No other candidates for office or referendums are to be voted on the same day.

All ballots are to be simple and the same for all the states. The voter has to sign in at the voting area.

The votes are to be counted by modern mechanical voting machines supplied to the towns and cities by the federal government... checked for accuracy before the election by a Federal election commission. The election commission is to have equal representation of the major political parties and the independent voter.

The winner will be the candidate with the most votes of the electoral college. The electoral college votes are to be distributed by Congressional District winners... no longer will there be a "winner take all" for the state. The winner of the statewide popular vote would get both Senatorial votes. States would not be overwhelmed by bloc votes in the cities. This would preserve the purposes of the electorial college.

All military overseas and absentee ballots must be postmarked and received and counted on election day.

2. CAMPAIGN FINANCE REFORM

This was one of the most heated issues discussed at the convention. The major corporations did not want limitations placed on their contributions. They were controlling the make-up of the congress. It became a class action fight. The rich were opposed to any changes, but the middle class and poor wanted controls. The poor won out because they controlled more votes. A limit for individuals and corporations was approved. It was one thousand dollars for individuals and five thousand dollars for corporations. The Amendment specified that no loopholes could be used to increase the amount.

Matching funds for the campaign for the Presidency is limited to 100 million dollars, a total of 200 million for each Party with a controlled inflationary clause for the future. There is to be four televised debates, one a month, starting four months before the election. A non-partisan election committee is to pick the location and moderators. The last session is to be an open forum with the questions to come from the audience. There are also provisions for an independent candidate to participate if he obtains ten percent of the vote. The contributions for candidates for Congress are limited to two million dollars and have to come from the state in which the candidate and corporation reside. The candidates could no longer get most of their money from out of state.

3. TERM LIMITS

The time had come for term limits because of the constant gridlock in the House of Representative and the Senate. The people wanted term limits but the incumbents in Congress were able to prevent the passage of an amendment to the Constitution. The majority of the states opposed the generations of lifelong wealthy politicians that their seniority imposed on the rest. Families and their offspring were the perennial candidates for Representative, Senator, or President. This was not what the forefathers wanted. Wealthy families should not inherit the National election offices of the United States of America. The Convention voted term limits for all states, so that a few states with perennial candidates would not dominate the chairmanships of the important committees. Members of the House of Representatives are limited to six terms of two years each. The Senate is limited to three six year terms.

4. THE RIGHT TO CARRY ARMS

Gun laws were changed and this was a surprise. AK rifles and rapid-fire guns were outlawed, including missile firing devices. Hunting rifles were all right, but not the rapid firing type. A Federal registration system for all guns was inaugurated. The waiting period was one month to obtain any gun. Handguns could only be used by police officers. Safety locks on handguns did not totally prevent homicides. There was a mandatory prison sentence for those who possessed handguns illegally. It was felt that the right to carry arms was important right after the Revolutionary War, to defend against aggressive nations and to obtain food to survive, but in today's society, it created a threat to all law-abiding citizens.

5. THE QUESTION OVER RIGHTS WAS ARGUED AND DEBATED

The right to privacy, to due process, to equal protection under the law was argued and debated. Computers were invading privacy and, in some cases, used maliciously and intentionally. The court system was also challenged regarding equal protection under the law. If you were wealthy and could afford the top lawyer or lawyers, was that equal protection if the poor man was assigned a fledgling lawyer for his defense – of course not! Laws were changed to pass this.

6. RIGHTS TO PRIVACY FOR THE PRESIDENT

Rights to privacy for the President were debated and passed. Since a man's home is his castle, and there are rights pertaining to that in the Constitution, the White House is the President's home during his term as President. Invasion of his privacy in his home is not warranted, and conversations of a secret nature between members of the President's staff, and cabinet members are protected as long as the conversations pertain to government business. The personal life of the President should be protected just as much as the personal life of any American citizen. The Secret Service could not testify about conversations with his staff unless they qualified for high crimes of a serious nature or unless they affected the function of the government.

7. A MEDICAL SUPREME COURT

Finally, and most importantly, the Constitutional Convention discussed and passed a new Medical Supreme Court. Its main purpose was to determine whether the President, Vice President, or members of Congress, Supreme Court, and Federal Courts were healthy enough to discharge the powers and duties of their said offices. The Medical Supreme Court was also to adjudicate all controversial major malpractice cases that had reached the district or appellate courts and were appealed.

AMENDMENTS THAT WERE PASSED
A Medical Supreme Court – Disability and Succession

CONSTITUTIONAL AMENDMENT 37

In order to adequately determine the removal of the President, Vice President, members of Congress, or members of the Supreme Court and Federal Judges from office for reasons of health demonstrated by their inability to discharge the powers and duties of their said offices.

A Medical Supreme Court made up of nine physicians and surgeons, representative of the people, will determine that disability. A vote of the majority of the Medical Supreme Court Justices is necessary for removal from office, and will be the highest jurisdiction in the land concerning disability and removal. The verdict of the Court is irrefutable and permanent.

The Medical Supreme Court Justices are to be representatives of the major medical societies in the U.S.A. and must be Amer-

ican citizens, born in the U.S.A. They are to be selected by a secret ballot of the members of each society when a vacancy develops. Three candidates for each medical society are to be selected by the members to be voted upon – one is elected to represent that society. If a vacancy occurs, a special election must take place within one month's time. The U.S. government is to oversee the balloting. There can be no discrimination based on race, ethnic group, or color.

One member from each society is to serve for one nine-year period. One-third of the members are to be replaced every three years. Age limit for serving on the Medical Supreme Court is seventy years of age. The Chief Justice is to be selected by a secret ballot of the nine sitting justices and his maximum term is six years.

The major medical societies that are to have one vote each are: Family practice, internal medicine, surgery, psychiatry, obstetrics and gynecology, orthopedics, pathology, radiology, and anesthesiology.

When a President is considered for disability, once the majority vote has been taken to remove, an immediate succession takes place. The line of succession to the Presidency must remain in the party that controls that office in this order after the Vice President; Senate Majority Leader, Speaker of the House, Secretary of State, Secretary of Defense, Secretary of the Treasury, Secretary of Health Education and Welfare and Secretary of Commerce.

If a member of Congress is voted to be removed, a state election to replace him must be held within three months. Supreme Court members (law and medicine) and Federal Court judges are not to serve beyond the age of seventy and their disability comes under the jurisdiction of the Medical Supreme Court.

The presentation of the disabled individual to the Court is to be done by selected physicians from the senior members of the three societies with the highest enrollment: Family practice, internal *medicine, and surgery. Three other senior members are to defend the disabled person.*

No media or photographic devices are allowed in the Medical Supreme Courtroom while the court is in session.

The President, Vice President, members of Congress, and the Supreme Court (judicial and medical) and Federal Courts must have a complete physical exam every six months or if evidence of a serious disability occurs, with all the findings released to the media and the press. Failure to do so calls for immediate removal from office. The National Institute of Health is to assign physicians to verify accuracy of the physical examinations.

The Medical Supreme Court will have the final jurisdiction over major malpractice cases that have been heard at the state district or appellate courts and then appealed. This includes major cases of environmental hazard or medical drugs or devices that impair the health of American citizens.

The Medical Supreme Court will also be consulted concerning controversial scientific laws that are difficult to interpret and the first Supreme Court (law) can request that they determine the legality.

6

MEDICAL SUPREME COURT

The changes in the Constitution made by the second Constitutional Convention were ratified by the legislatures of three-fourths of the States. Most states called special sessions of the legislature to expedite the passage. The Congress could do nothing to stop it.

The most controversial part of the 37th Amendment (Succession and Disability) was the age limit placed on the Supreme Court Justices and the annual physical examination with disclosure of the findings to the public. It was all-inclusive – the President, Vice President, Congress and the Supreme and Federal Court Justices.

Kelli was in excellent health as was her Vice President, Brian Hatfield. Some of the members of Congress and Supreme Court Justices were hedging on having the physical exam with disclosure, but when they realized they would be removed from office if they didn't, they acquiesced. After all, the new Constitution was the law of the land and they had to abide by it.

There were some big surprises. One of the Supreme Court Justices (law), 77 years of age, had evidence of a neurological deficit and when the CAT scan and MRI were done of his head, they showed an undetected brain tumor in the frontal lobe. Because it involved the frontal lobe, there was no outward noticeable defect, although he complained of headaches. His reaction time was slow on some of the court cases, but his written opinions were excellent, because he had a top staff of law clerks.

Another Supreme Court Justice had advanced heart disease and was periodically having evidence of light-headedness and dizziness. The heart pump wasn't pushing enough blood to his brain. It was determined that he was also throwing off small emboli to his brain from his heart with periodic T.I.A.s (transient ischemic attacks).

Once the evidence was released to the public, both of the Supreme Court Justices resigned, rather than go before the Medical Supreme Court.

All sorts of unusual health findings were showing up in the members of Congress. Four senior members had previously undetected cancer at various stages of involvement. They hadn't had a good physical for two or three years. Three members had advanced liver disease (cirrhosis) secondary to hepatitis or alcoholism; two female members had undetected breast cancer, and two male members were found to have colon cancer after a colonoscopy was done.

Most of the members of Congress were pleased with the mandatory physical examination, because it was all-inclusive. It forced them to see a doctor. If you were really in bad health, or had a potential life-threatening disease, you really weren't serving the best interests of your country by staying in office.

The most difficult part of implementing the changes approved at the second Constitutional Convention and added to the original Constitution, was determining the make-up of the members of the new Medical Supreme Court. They were to be selected by the doctors of the various medical societies by secret ballot of their members -- the balloting monitored by the Federal Government.

Although there was a lot of politicking that went on in the various medical societies as they selected their candidates, when the dust settled, it was amazing that the various medical societies had selected a diverse group of doctors with excellent academic backgrounds -- there were two Blacks, one Hispanic, one Asian and five Whites selected – four were women.

The Chief Justice of the Medical Supreme Court was selected by secret ballot of the members of the Court. He was Dr, Mark Jackson, a Black from Washington, D.C. Mark had a national reputation and a very high I.Q. When he was a juvenile, he graduated from high school at the age of twelve and then attended Georgia Tech University, graduating at fifteen. He then went to Harvard where he received a double degree in medicine and law at the age of 21.

He decided that he wanted to become a surgeon so he took a residency in surgery at John's Hopkins University. When he completed his residency, he joined the academic attending staff at Howard University in Washington, D.C. In a short period of time, he became the Chief of Surgery, at the ripe old age of 31 years. He was a prolific researcher and writer and edited three textbooks on surgery, including one on breast disease. Because of his law degree, he was often asked to be a medical witness in major malpractice cases around the country. His intellect, photographic memory and legal background made him a formidable opponent for the opposing attorneys.

Eventually, in major controversial cases, because of frequent coverage by the media, Mark became a national celebrity. He did not hesitate to oppose leading academic medical specialists in the courtroom if they did something wrong. At the age of forty, he was presented with an unusual challenge. He received a phone call from one of the most prestigious law firms in New York City – Clarkson, Bailey, Constanza, Patria and English. Attorney Jack Bailey, a senior partner called him on the phone.

"Mark, this is Attorney Jack Bailey. You've reviewed some cases for us in the past. We're having difficulty with a malpractice case that we're involved with and would like you to help us."

"Is it in trial?"

"No, but it's on the docket in three weeks. Our expert witness had a severe heart attack last week and he's out of it. He's going to have by-pass surgery. You're name was suggested."

"I'd like to help you, but I'm extremely busy right now. I'm involved with the American College of Surgeons meeting coming up in San Francisco. Why do you specifically want me?"

"Because it's a breast cancer malpractice case, and I understand that you wrote a classic book about breast cancer. We did a computer search about the case, and you wrote a chapter on the subject involved in the litigation."

"Sometimes, I wish that I hadn't written that book. It's gotten me involved in all sorts of controversy."

"Well you got involved and you're good at it."

"Getting time to do it, is my problem. Is it for the plaintiff or the doctor?"

"The plaintiff – a twenty-five year old women who is dying from breast cancer."

"Sounds interesting. I'll tell you what. I was going to do some skiing this weekend. Fax the material to me here in D.C., and I'll read the brief. Have there been any discovery depositions so far?"

"Yes, there have. That's why we need you."

"Well, I have one rule. If the facts suggest malpractice, I'll take the case. You may have to stall for my appearance in court, however."

"I think we can do that."

"What part of the country is involved?"

"Atlanta, Georgia."

"I'm Black, you know."

"We know that. We're not interested in your color. We're interested in your brain."

Mark received the material by over-night mail. The law firm didn't want to put it on the fax because they wanted strict confidentiality. Mark took the material and drove to his beach retreat home near Ocean City, Maryland. It turned out to be a rainy weekend, so he relaxed in a big leather chair in his study and read the material.

Mary Bell Jensen
Plaintiff
vs
Jack Marshall, M.D.
George Perkins, M.D.
Defendants

The plaintiff was Mary Bell Jensen, a 25-year-old white woman who lived in a community outside of Atlanta, Georgia. She felt a small lump under her left nipple and went to see her obstetrician Jack Marshall about it.

"I've got a small lump under my left nipple," she replied. "It's the size of a pea. I'm worried about it because my mother died of breast cancer."

"Well," replied the obstetrician. "Even before I examine you, I can tell you that cancer of the breast in your age group is non-existent. Where did you feel this lump?"

"Under my left nipple?"

The obstetrician proceeded to examine her left nipple, briefly squeezing the nipple. A little cheesy material came out.

"It's nothing. It's a plugged milk duct."

"Thank goodness," replied the patient. "Is there anything I should do about it?"

"You can soak in a warm tub if you like. The heat may make it disappear faster."

"Thanks," she replied.

"Just because your mother had breast cancer, doesn't mean that you're going to get it," replied the doctor. "Relax!"

Two months later, the lump got bigger and there was no discharge. She noted that both breasts were getting larger and she missed her period. She did a pregnancy test on herself and found out that she was pregnant. She returned to her obstetrician.

"That lump in my left breast has gotten bigger."

"That's because you're pregnant."

"What should I do?"

"Really nothing, or you can put some warm soaks on your breast. You'll be coming in regularly now because you're pregnant. I'll keep an eye on it."

Three months later, she went back to her ob-gyn. The lump had gotten bigger and was about the size of a pigeon's egg. When she was examined, she took his hand and had him feel the lump.

"I'm worried about that lump."

"You're breasts are bigger because you're pregnant and that's why it feels much larger. It feels cystic to me."

"Because of my mom, I worry about it all the time."

"Well, if it makes you feel better, I'll send you to a surgeon, George Perkins."

"Thanks, that would be helpful," she replied.

A week later, she went to the surgeon who examined her breasts. She told him about her mother and about her breast lump. He examined both of her breasts and under her armpits.

"You have a small lump in your left breast," Perkins replied. "Your breasts are quite large from your pregnancy. I believe you have what we call a fibroadenoma – a small solid tumor."

"Can it be malignant?"

"No, never. We'll take it out after you have your baby. You'll be fine."

At seven months of her pregnancy, the patient developed a painful hemorrhoid and a nurse practitioner in the obstetrician's office gave her the name of a proctologist to see. She went to see Dr. George Speirs. He did a brief physical on her, blood pressure, listened to her heart and then felt her breasts.

"Young lady, you have a lump in your left breast. It feels hard. You should have that taken out."

"I've already seen somebody about that, another surgeon."

"Good," he replied. "Get it out!"

The proctologist put her legs up in stirrups and injected the thrombosed hemorrhoid area with a local anesthetic and then drained it and then tied off the base of the dilated vein. He put her on antibiotics and gave her pain medication. She had no further rectal problems. She decided to rely on the decision of the first surgeon about her breast. She'd have it taken care of after she had her baby.

She gave birth to a healthy 9 lb., 11-oz boy at term without any major complications, and went back to her ob-gyn doctor, Dr. Marshall, one week later and told him that she wanted to breast-feed her baby. She reminded him about the lump.

"You can breast-feed for a few months and then have your surgeon take that fibroadenoma out," he replied.

Three months later, the patient and her husband took a vacation for a week around the Pensacola, Florida area and her husband commented about the lump in her left breast. It was quite noticeable when he saw her in the nude coming out of the shower.

"When are you going to have that thing taken out?" he asked.

"Soon," she replied. "It's nothing to worry about."

The next day they were driving to the beach and there was a big sign on a building that said, Pensacola Breast Diagnostic Clinic – Walk-ins Accepted. She decided to go in.

A young doctor examined her.

"My God Lady! Where have you been with this big lump?"

"I've already seen a gynecologist and a surgeon." She then related her entire history.

"I can't believe it! I'll do a mammogram right now. In fact, it should have been done when you first felt the lump. You could have protected the baby from x-rays with a lead shield, you know."

The mammogram was done and revealed a large 5 cm. solid tumor, the size of a tennis ball in her left breast. It had a star-like stellate appearance. There also were enlarged glands under her left armpit. Under local anesthesia, a needle biopsy was done on the lump in her breast. It revealed an aggressive cancer.

She immediately went to a large breast cancer center and saw a cancer team comprised of radiologists, medical oncologists and surgeons. They advised her to have chemotherapy followed by surgery and radiation. She refused and replied:

"I can't stand knowing that that big lump is full of cancer. I want it cut out right away! I want to be around for my baby."

She insisted on surgery, so a mastectomy and removal of some axillary glands were done. All the glands removed from under her armpit were positive. She received post-operative radiation and chemotherapy and six months later developed headaches followed by convulsions. A MRI Brain Scan revealed diffuse involvement of her bones, chest and brain. Her chest x-ray had been negative prior to her mastectomy.

On Monday, when Mark got back to Washington, D.C. he called the New York Law Firm and spoke to Attorney Jack Bailey.

"I reviewed the case you sent me this past weekend. It's an obvious case of malpractice and I don't think it should go to trial."

"They've already set the trial date. It's five weeks from now."

"Who's their expert?"

"They have two experts. One's from a cancer center in Texas, Dr. Todd Wilkins, and the other from a cancer center in Buffalo, Dr. George Shawberg. Because of the amount of money involved, it will be tried in the Superior Court in Atlanta, Georgia.

"I can't believe it. Something's drastically wrong."

"You're right! To get those two experts, it's going to cost them big bucks."

"Well, I'll take the case. Justice has to be served. The gynecologist and the surgeon both committed malpractice. A mammogram, needle biopsy, or open biopsy with no risk to the patient should have been done at two to four months, and she'd be alive and well today. The case is well documented and it's obvious malpractice."

"Good. I hoped that you'd take the case. The defense lawyers will want to do a discovery or deposition to evaluate you and your reasons. I'll keep in touch and notify you when it will take place."

The deposition took place in Mark's office in Washington, D.C. Both law firms agreeing to the location. The main theme for the defense that came out in the deposition was that the rarity of the cancer in a 25-year-old pregnant woman should excuse the doctors for missing the diagnosis. Mark couldn't believe it. He knew that the most common type of cancer during a pregnancy was breast cancer. As for the rarity argument, that was ridiculous! If you practice medicine you have to keep up with the current literature and they had not.

A month later, the date for the trial arrived and the date for Mark's interrogation soon followed. He would be giving his opinion on a Monday morning in the Superior Court in Atlanta, Georgia, and the defense would ask him questions in the afternoon.

The Superior Court Judge in the case was the Honorable John Cassidy who had been on the bench for over fifteen years. He was a Stanford Law School graduate.

In the beginning, the trial lawyer for the plaintiff went over Mark's background, which was impeccable with very little challenge by the defense attorneys. The defense had three different insurance company lawyers working together and the lead defense lawyer was a 50-year-old redhead, Attorney James Andrews, who was a nationally recognized malpractice trial lawyer.

The courtroom was packed with numerous media present. Mark gave his reasons why malpractice had been committed and refuted some of the defenses arguments that were brought up in the deposition. He stated that the gynecologist and the surgeon who saw the patient should not be excused because they did not conform to the practice habits and methods of modern day physicians.

He really dropped a bombshell in the courtroom when he presented material from a chapter in his breast textbook about pregnancy and cancer. The trial lawyer he was working with, brought out a big graph to show to the jury... the defense immediately objected.

"This material was not presented to us at a deposition taken in D.C., Your Honor. It should not be submitted as evidence and should not be seen by the jury."

"Very well," said Judge Cassidy. "Excuse the jury."

When they left the room, the Judge turned to Mark and asked, "Just what do those statistics and figures mean on that large graph?"

"Your Honor, the defense has been trying to prove that the patient's cancer was so rare that the doctors taking care of her should be excused. Also the tumor was so advanced that she would have died anyway when she developed her cancer... therefore, she should receive no compensation. Those figures on that graph show a complete study done by me. The material was taken from one of the best tumor registries in the country about breast cancer and pregnancy in women under the age of 30 years.

There were over two hundred cases with a 65 percent five-year survival rate. It also shows that if you detect breast cancer when it is small or tiny, such as small microcalcifications, that are the size of a pinhead, you can get almost a 90% cure-rate. This patient would have survived if the doctors involved had done a needle biopsy, open biopsy, or a mammogram early on in her disease. If they had listened to the patient in the beginning, and it's all in the record, she described it as being "pea size", she'd be alive today."

The defense lawyer immediately jumped to his feet. 'Your Honor, we would like to ask Dr. Jackson about those statistics and that graph."

The Judge hit the gavel down. "Court is recessed for lunch. You can ask the questions after lunch."

After lunch, it was the defense's turn to question Mark. Jim Andrews, the redheaded trial lawyer was hot under the collar because of his inability to question Mark about his chart on breast cancer statistics related to pregnancy. He knew that those statistics were valid because they were taken from the oldest and most reputable tumor registry in the United States. He went up to where Mark was sitting near the bench and said, "Do you know anything about computers?"

"A little," he replied.

"I have a small computer here in my hand. Do you recognize it?"

"Yes."

"How many women under 30 that were pregnant, have you taken care of with breast cancer?"

"Five or six, I believe."

"How many cancer patients have you seen during your life-time?"

"I don't know. Maybe thirty or forty thousand."

"How many breast cancer patients under 30 years were on that chart that you showed before lunch?"

The plaintiff's lawyer stood up. "Objection, Your Honor. The jury was unable to see that chart."

"Objection sustained."

"I've put all these numbers on this computer. It shows you how rare breast cancer in pregnancy is. Please read it for the jurors.

"I agree, it's infinitesimal but any hard lump in a woman's breast should be investigated. No matter what her age.

"Why are you implicating the surgeon in this malpractice case?"

"Because he felt a lump and said she had a fibroadenoma... a solid tumor. You can't make a diagnosis using your fingers on a pregnant breast! It's like using a crystal ball to determine the outcome. He should have done a mammogram, a needle biopsy or an open biopsy."

"What's the doubling time of a cancer?"

"It is the time that it takes a cancer cell to reduplicate itself."

"Was this breast cancer a stage III advanced cancer when the patient first discovered it? Did it involve the glands under her armpit? Had it spread from the nipple area?"

"No, because when she first felt it, she describes it as being pea shaped in size. Her examining doctors, the gynecologist and surgeon, did not describe involvement of the glands under her armpits in their charts. That meant that it was still localized to the breast. It was small. The size of a tumor determines the approximate percentage of cases that will spread (metastasize). In all likelihood, this cancer had not spread when she first felt it and told her doctor about it. It was in it's infancy... a Stage I cancer."

"Can you determine the doubling time of this patient's tumor?"

"Yes. You can approximate it. I can do that in my head if you like."

"No further questions. Mark's intelligence and mindset had overwhelmed the defense lawyers.

Six weeks later, Mark had his secretary call the trial lawyer in Atlanta to get the results.

"The trial lawyer wants to talk to you on the phone," said his secretary.

"Dr. Jackson, you can't believe what happened. The two so-called breast experts from Texas and Buffalo backed out of the case when they read your deposition taken by the defense law firm. One had written a textbook on breast cancer and the other was chairman of a surgical department. They refused to testify. They did not want to be sued for perjury. Judge Cassidy directed a verdict for the plaintiff. He didn't allow the jury to vote. The case settled for over a million dollars. I'm sure he felt the jury would support the local doctors. You did a great job. Thanks for your excellent testimony."

The New York Times, Washington Post and the Los Angeles Times carried a complete transcript of Mark Jackson's testimony in Atlanta. Breast cancer was a national issue and breast cancer in pregnancy had not been discussed in an open forum. The judge, the trial lawyers and the so-called expert witnesses for the defense were all under the spotlight glare of the news media. When the national experts for the defense from Texas and Buffalo withdrew from the case, they had trouble finding someone to testify. They finally put two local general surgeons on the stand. It didn't work. Judge Cassidy realized what they were doing so he directed the verdict. The public was very impressed by Dr. Mark Jackson and he was overwhelmed by the publicity he created. Both political parties suggested that he run for public office.

Howard University Medical School

All was not well with Howard University Medical School and their surgical chief. He was called on more frequently for malpractice cases, which kept him out of the operating room. In order to teach surgery properly, the Chief of Surgery has to get into the surgical arena to teach residents the proper skills of a good surgeon. He's supposed to be a top operating surgeon. This can be time consuming and Mark was spending a lot of time in the courtroom. He realized this and felt that he had spent over ten years in teaching in the surgical field and thought that the legal profession needed help in the medical-legal realm. It would be a new challenge.

He sent a letter of resignation to the Dean of Howard University Medical School and then started a new law firm in Washington, D.C. He recruited a top group of lawyers and it wasn't long before the law firm became one of the busiest in the Washington, D.C. area.

Mark got involved in many cases before the Supreme Court and there was talk that he would make a great Supreme Court Judge.

When the second Constitutional Convention was convened and they passed the amendment to form the Medical Supreme Court, Mark's peers felt that his knowledge of the legal law and his knowledge of correlated medical problems would make him an ideal candidate to become a member of the new Medical Supreme Court. The American College of Surgeons agreed, and he was selected to represent the surgeons on the Medical Supreme Court.

7

A WOMAN JURIST

Some of the other medical societies had difficulties in selecting their candidates for the Medical Supreme Court. More and more women were now going to medical school to become doctors, many going into the obstetric-gynecology field to practice. They wanted a woman to represent them on the Medical Supreme Court. One of their strongest candidates for the job was Attorney Maria Sanchez from San Diego, a Mexican American.

Maria's mother, a single, young Mexican wanted her child to become an American citizen. When she was nine months pregnant and ready to deliver, she was smuggled into the U.S.A. near San Diego and two days later, gave birth to her daughter in an emergency room. Because Maria was born in the U.S.A., she became an American citizen and her mother started working in San Diego as a nanny for a wealthy businessman with two small children. She was a live-in nanny with her child and they both quickly learned English. Soon they were accepted as equals within the family.

Maria was very bright and excelled in her studies. Because of her grades she received a full scholarship to the University of California in Berkley and then went on to Stanford Medical School. She took a residency at UCLA and a fellowship in gynecology-oncology at Memorial Sloan Kettering in New York City. Maria was made the Chief of the Ob-Gyn service at UCLA seven years later, and then got politically involved in arguments about abortion rights. She was opposed to abortions after three months and felt that the government should subsidize the cost for young women who got pregnant but couldn't afford the costs of carrying the baby to term. She was getting nowhere with her arguments because she was a doctor. She began giving some serious thought to becoming a lawyer.

After ten years in practice, she returned to college and went to Stanford Law School and became a lawyer, active in the local political arena. She was frequently consulted for medical malpractice cases because of her background and was also being considered for political office.

Maria had an excellent fellowship in gynecology cancer surgery when she was at Memorial Sloan Kettering Hospital in New York City. She scrubbed on many radical surgical procedures and because of this, learned the anatomy of the pelvis perfectly. This gave her an intellectual independence when she operated. Cervical cancer had improved remarkably because of early detection but ovarian cancer was still a serious problem, with many of the patients presenting with advanced cancer when first detected. When doing a pelvic examination through the vagina, it was difficult to feel the ovaries with a finger and other means of detection were needed such as transvaginal ultrasound and color doppler studies. If there was an unusual change in the appearance of the ovary on the ultrasound, an exploratory-laporascopic procedure could be done through a small abdominal incision to get a direct look at the ovaries. Biopsy of the ovary under direct fiberoptic visualization expedited the diagnosis. CA 125 blood tests were available and were helpful sometimes, but were not totally diagnostic.

Lori Karp
Plaintiff
vs.
William Pruett, M.D.
Defendant

It wasn't long before Maria was asked to be an expert witness in a high profile ovarian cancer case. The patient was the daughter of one of California's Senators in Washington, D.C. The Senator was mad as hell about a delay in her daughter's diagnosis. She contacted a nationally known law firm; Baldwin, DePalo, Stuart and Sussman that had offices in San Francisco, Chicago, and Washington, D.C. Attorney Gene Stuart agreed to take the case. He made a phone call to Dr. Maria Sanchez.

"Dr. Sanchez, this is Attorney Gene Stuart on the phone. I understand that you're an attorney, also. Our law firm would like you to be an expert witness in a malpractice case for us."

"What type of case is it?"

"Delay in diagnosis in ovarian cancer."

"Is it for the patient or is it defending the doctor?"

"It's for the patient."

"Is it a realistic law suit or a frivolous case to make money? In other words, is it legitament?"

"We think so."

"Send me all the material you have with complete hospital records and I'll review it. If it's legitimate, I'll do it."

The next day, Maria received a box of hospital records and depositions taken from the patient and the doctors involved. The doctor being sued was a prominent gynecological cancer surgeon who had trained at a cancer center in Buffalo, New York and was a full professor at UCLA.

On the following weekend, Maria read the voluminous material.

The patient was Lori Karp, a 50-yar-old white female who had worked as a medical secretary for a prominent surgeon for twenty-five years. She had two children and because she had two aunts who had died from ovarian cancer, was being seen every six months by the gynecological cancer surgeon, Dr. William Pruett. He would do a pelvic examination and order a pelvic ultrasound study of her ovaries. Past history was significant in that she had her uterus removed for persistent vaginal bleeding, at the age of 34 years… her ovaries were not removed… her appendix was. All of her tests were essentially normal until the age of forty-eight when she went to see her doctor with abdominal pain.

"I haven't been feeling too good lately," she said. "I've had some intermittent abdominal pain on my right side."

"Have you had a fever?"

"No."

"Bowel movements okay?"

"Yes."

"When did you have your last ultrasound?"

"Four months ago."

Dr. Pruitt did a pelvic exam and felt no tenderness or abnormalities. "It might be that you have adhesions where your appendix was removed."

"I can live with that," said Lori.

"I'll order an ultrasound," said Pruitt.

Lori requested that a copy of her report be sent to her boss, Dr. Paul Scott. She read the report when it came into his office.

'Left ovary appears normal. Right ovary has what appears to be a cystic enlargement not seen before. Suggest re-exam and close follow-up.'

She showed the report to her boss, Dr. Scott.

"Get your ovaries out, Lori, so that you don't have to worry about cancer. You're menopausal now. They're not doing you any good and you have a family history of ovarian cancer."

When Lori went back to see Dr. Pruitt, she told him what Dr. Scott said.

"What does he know about women's problems? I've looked at those x-rays! All you've got is a small cyst. Besides, removing the ovaries doesn't protect against getting ovarian cancer. Don't listen to your boss!"

Two years later, Lori felt lousy again and her right lower quadrant abdominal pain returned. She decided to go back to see Dr. Pruitt.

"I've got that pain again," Lori said.

"When did you have your last pelvic ultrasound?"

"Five months ago."

Dr. Pruitt did another pelvic exam.

"Everything's fine down below. Don't be such a worrywart. Women get strange symptoms when they go through the menopause."

Lori continued to feel lousy. The surgeon she worked for was in Florida for two weeks. He finally returned and as usual he was overbooked because he had been away. He noticed that Lori didn't look well.

"Lori, you look awfully tired. Maybe you should have gone on vacation instead of me."

"I feel lousy. I've been having some pain in my right lower abdomen. I saw Dr. Pruitt three weeks ago and was checked. He said that everything was all right. I know it isn't. Would you examine me?"

"When we get through today, have Karen set you up in one of the rooms. I'll do a pelvic exam. Take a Fleet's enema first."

When Dr. Scott examined Lori, he couldn't believe what he found. She had a huge grapefruit-sized mass on the right side and the rest of her pelvis was fixed and hard. When he examined her belly, he felt an apron-like mass in her upper abdomen that was tender.

Lori watched Dr. Scott's eyes and face as he examined her. He didn't have to tell her that she was in big trouble. There were tears in her eyes.

"We're going to do a CT scan of your abdomen, stat, tomorrow... Karen get me the Chief of Radiology on the phone."

The next day, the CT Scan was done and it showed two enlarged abnormal ovaries, fluid in the abdomen, and a 10 cm. x 8 cm. mass involving the upper abdominal omentum (the apron over the bowel). Lori had an advanced Stage 3 to 4 ovarian cancer with spread throughout her abdomen.

In the past, Lori would have been called inoperable. She might have a look into her abdomen by a surgeon... an exploratory laparatomy, but then closed up. The modern approach is to debulk the tumor, remove as much as possible, and then give expensive anti-tumor agents... Lori cried uncontrollably when she heard the news.

"You need an operation to try to take most of that tumor out, Lori. I'm going to call Dr. Pruitt and blast the hell out of him. What was he doing when he examined you? He must have had his head up his ass!"

Lori looked at Dr. Scott with tears in her eyes. "I'm going to die... I know it... aren't I?... I want to live as long as I can... my daughter has a little four month old boy... my first and only grandchild."

"When you're operated on, I'll be in the operating room, all day if need be," said Dr. Scott.

"Thanks, I'd like that."

The news about Lori's illness traveled around the hospital. One of the young surgeons that Dr. Scott had trained, and had worked in his office, stopped him in the hallway.

"I've heard about your secretary Lori… I'm sorry. Who's going to operate on her?"

"Dr. Pruitt."

"Oh! That's bad!"

"What' ya mean?"

"Dr. Pruitt operated on my wife for a routine hysterectomy two years ago. She almost bled to death on the table. While dissecting around the uterus, he accidentally cut into her ileac vein, a big vein in the pelvis. She lost six pints of blood and was bleeding to death… one of the vascular surgeons had to come in and control the bleeding."

"You've got to be kidding me?"

"It's true."

"Thanks. I'll get Dr. Jack Bern, the surgical oncologist from Johns Hopkins to scrub in on her case."

"Pruitt won't like it."

"He doesn't have a choice," said Scott.

Lori was placed on a bowel prep, had blood studies, and was seen by anesthesia. Three days later, at 8:00 AM, she was wheeled into the operating room and put to sleep. Her boss, had scrubbed up and put a mask and gown on, to observe.

After the patient was prepped and draped, Dr. Pruitt and his chief resident started the operation… a small lower mid-abdominal incision. Within minutes they were inside the abdominal cavity and Pruitt put his gloved hand inside and then proclaimed; "She's totally inoperable, everything's stuck. We'll close her up."

Dr. Scott standing below the table said; "Like hell you will! Open her all the way up! You can't see through that little opening." He then turned to the circulating nurse and said; "Call Dr. Bern and tell him to get his ass in here, pronto!"

Dr. Bern soon arrived, scrubbed up and joined the team. It was obvious that the case was too big for Pruitt to handle. Dr. Bern took over the operating position and began dissecting the large mass off the upper colon. He dissected, meticulously, in order to avoid entering the bowel and causing spillage. Pruitt assisted Bern. Bern successfully took the mass out.

"Why don't you take over and take the ovaries out?" said Bern to Pruitt.

"Okay," he replied as they changed places at the operating table. After a short while, Bern noticed that Pruitt's hands were shaking and he appeared extremely nervous. He also was lost in the anatomy because of the distortion caused by the tumor.

"I'd better do it," said Bern. "Give me the scissors." Pruitt gladly turned them over to him.

"We better find the ureters first... don't want to cut them... don't want piss all over the belly," he said as he dissected above the pelvis. He soon found a sausage-shaped tube. Her left ureter was dilated above the tumor. He placed a hard tube in the ureter and then dissected above it and removed the left ovary. The right side wasn't obstructed and he was able to find the right ureter easily. He then removed the right ovary. About 95% of the visible tumor was removed by Dr. Bern.

Lori survived the operation and once her wound was healed, saw a female medical oncologist, Dr. Norma Stone. Dr. Scott went with her for her first evaluation and treatment.

"Lori, you're not going to die for quite a while," said Stone. "Put that out of your mind! We have new medicine for treating ovarian cancer. You'll live comfortably for at least three to five years. Get ahold of yourself and stop crying."

"What about losing my hair and being sick?"

"You will get nauseated and will get tired. We have new medicines to control that. You'll have a finger stick once a week to check your blood. We'll be giving you Taxol intravenously and carboplatinum, once a week for six to eight weeks, as an outpatient. You will lose your hair, so we'll get you a wig. Do you have any questions?"

"No."

Lori got deathly ill with nausea and vomiting and the dry heaves with her first treatment. Stone had to adjust her dosage. The fatigue was overwhelming and after three treatments, her red cell and white cell blood count got very low and did not respond to medication -- her platelet count that helps clot blood, got dangerously low. She had to receive a platelet transfusion.

After Lori's sixth treatment with Taxol, Lori got deathly ill. Her white blood count went down to one thousand and her hemoglobin and red cells dropped precipitously. She was out of it and bordering on completely cracking mentally. She was desperately ill and looked like a white wax doll without any rouge.

"I can't take it any more! A can't stand it!" she said, crying like a baby. Dr. Stone tried to reassure her and gave her a strong mood elevator pill but it didn't work. It was obvious that the tumor was not responding. A CT scan showed multiple areas of partial bowel obstruction. Dr. Stone agreed to try something else… Topotecan and an experimental drug.

Lori wasn't eating and knew she was losing ground… losing the fight.

She talked to Dr. Scott about suing Dr. Pruitt.

"No woman should go through what I'm going through… Dr. Pruitt did not do his job right! I want you to help me document what's happening. I'm not going to be around very long to testify against him. Would you get me a lawyer?"

"I will, cause I agree with you," said Dr. Scott.

Dr. Scott knew about Dr. Maria Sanchez and had worked with her when she was a practicing gynecologist. He called her law office and she agreed to see Lori. After seeing her, she immediately instituted a medical malpractice lawsuit against Dr. William Pruitt in the Superior Court, Judicial District of San Diego. Dr. Pruitt retained the services of the law firm, Ryan, Reed, Millbrook and DeLuca.

Because Attorney Sanchez realized that Lori could die rapidly at any time, she arranged for a video to be made that might be used in a courtroom, if necessary.

She also asked the court to appoint a judge as soon as possible, to rule on procedures. Judge Robert Daylin was named and the defense tried to prevent a preliminary hearing from taking place... stating that they needed more time to document the case and to obtain expert witnesses and prepare their defense. Their plan was to delay as long as possible so that Lori would not be in the courtroom when the trial took place.

At the preliminary hearing, Judge Daylin ruled that the patient should be deposed as soon as possible. The case was moved up on the court's docket. Finally, the defense deposed Lori.

THE GENERAL COURT OF JUSTICE
SUPERIOR COURT DIVISION
San Diego
California

Lori Karp
Plaintiff
vs.
William Pruett, M.D.
Defendant

DEPOSITION OF LORI KARP

APPEARANCES:

For the Plaintiff
Cole, Turner, Sanchez and Fischer
By: Maria Sanchez, Esq.

For the Defendant
Ryan, Reed, Milbrook and DeLuca
By: Jack Reed, Esq.

Susan K. Johnson
certified legal transcriber

The deposition took place at the law offices of Ryan, Reed, Milbrook and DeLuca.

The witness, after having first been duly sworn to tell the truth, the whole truth, and nothing but the truth, was examined and testified as follows:

By: <u>Mr. Jack Reed</u>

Q. Would you state your name, please.

A. Lori Karp.

Q. How old are you?

A. Fifty years old.

Q. Where were you born?

A. San Diego, California.

Q. How far did you go in school?

A. I graduated from High School and went to secretarial school for one year and six months at Katherine Gibbs.

Q. Where have you worked?

A. I worked at an insurance company for five years and 25 years for Dr. Paul Scott.

Q. Do you have children?

A. Yes, two daughters.

Q. Tell me about your health background.

A. I had a hysterectomy at 35 years for prolonged vaginal bleeding and other than that, have been in good health.

Q. Lori, how long did Dr. William Pruitt take care of you?

A. Eight years.

Q. Did he do a good history and physical exam when he saw you?

Q. I thought so. I told him that I had two aunts that died from ovarian cancer.

Q. What was his response?

A: We'll have to keep a close eye on you.

Q. What tests did he do?

A. Pelvic exam and ultrasound studies of my ovaries every six months.

Q. Did Dr. Pruitt go over all the tests with you?

A. Yes. However, I had a copy sent to the surgeon I worked for.

Q. Did you see any other doctors about your problems?

A. No. I trusted Dr. Pruitt.

Q. When you got sick two years later and went to see Dr. Pruitt, what did you tell him?

A. I told him that I had been intermittently sick for three months with cramping abdominal pain.

Q. What was his response?

A. He blamed it on menopausal changes.

Q. Were you still menstruating?

A. No. My uterus was out.

Q. When did you talk to Dr. Scott about you problems?

A. When he got back from Florida.

Q. Why did you tell Dr. Scott about your problems?

A. Because I trusted him. I watched him take care of his patients.

Q. Why didn't you have your ovaries taken out?

A. Because Dr. Pruitt told me that it wouldn't prevent me from getting ovarian cancer.

Q. That's all the questions.

THE GENERAL COURT OF JUSTICE
SUPERIO.R. COURT DIVISION
San Diego
California

Lori Karp
Plaintiff
vs.
William Pruett, M.D.
Defendant

DEPOSITION OF PAUL SCOTT, M.D.

A P P E A R A N C E S:

For the Plaintiff
Cole, Turner, Sanchez and Fischer
By: Maria Sanchez, Esq.

For the Defendant
Ryan, Reed, Milbrook and DeLuca
By: William Ryan, Esq.

Kathy Jones
certified legal transcriber

The deposition took place at the law offices of Ryan, Reed, Milbrook and DeLuca.

The witness, after having first been duly sworn to tell the truth, the whole truth, and nothing but the truth, was examined and testified as follows:

By: <u>Attorney Ryan</u>

Q: How long has Lori Karp worked for you?

A: Twenty-five years. She started working part-time and eventually was my top employee. She's a great secretary.

Q. Has she ever been sick before?

A. When she was 35-years-old, she had some abnormal vaginal bleeding from her uterus and had a hysterectomy – ovaries were not taken out.

Q. Did she receive routine sick days?

A. Yes, but she never used them. She accumulated them and was either paid extra or used them for vacation time.

Q. When did you notice that there was a change?.. that she was sick.

A. I took a two week vacation in Florida and when I got back, she looked horrible… it wasn't like her at all.

Q. Did you examine her?

A. Yes. She asked me to. She had seen Dr. Pruitt three weeks before and he told her that he could find nothing wrong.

Q. Had you examined Lori before?

A. No. If the girls in my office have health problems, I'd refer them to whom I think are the best doctors.

Q. When you examined Lori, what did you find?

A. She had a fixed, solid pelvis with a mass on her right side. Nothing was soft and pliable. I could also feel a mass in her belly. I ordered a CT Scan. The rest is history.

Q. Do you feel that you can get a good examination of the ovaries by feeling with your fingers way up in the pelvis?

A. It's tough sometimes if the patient's obese. Lori is not.

Q. When do you do an ultrasound?

A. When the patient presents with symptoms or if she's in a risk group.

Q. Is there anything else you can do?

A. You can do CA 125 blood tests. It measures a protein that's elevated in ovarian cancer. If the patient is young, childbearing, and wants to save their ovaries, you can take a look inside the belly and biopsy the ovaries by using a laporoscope.

Q. Shouldn't you feel something first?

A. No. Not if she has risk factors and the ultrasound suggests an abnormality.

THE GENERAL COURT OF JUSTICE
SUPERIOR. COURT DIVISION
San Diego
California

Lori Karp
Plaintiff
vs.
William Pruett, M.D.
Defendant

DEPOSITION OF WILLIAM PRUITT, M.D.

A P P E A R A N C E S:

For the Plaintiff
Cole, Turner, Sanchez and Fischer
By: Maria Sanchez, Esq.

For the Defendant
Ryan, Reed, Milbrook and DeLuca
By: Jack Reed, Esq.

Patricia Smith
certified legal transcriber.

The deposition took place at the law offices of Ryan, Reed, Milbrook and DeLuca.

The witness, after having first been duly sworn to tell the truth, the whole truth, and nothing but the truth, was examined and testified as follows:

By: Maria Sanchez, Esq.

Q: <u>Attorney Sanchez</u>: Dr. Pruitt, please state your Medical educational background.

A: <u>Dr. Pruitt</u>: I graduated from Yale undergrad and Harvard medical and took an Obstretrical-Gynecological residency at Boston Women's Hospital. I then took a one-year Oncology-Gynecology fellowship in Cancer in Buffalo.

Q. How long have you taken care of Lori Karp?

A. Eight years.

Q. Describe what sort of a history and physical examination you do on your patients.

A. A complete comprehensive history and physical exam each year. In Lori Karp's case, a pelvic exam and ultrasound every six months.

Q. Did you bring Lori Karp's office records with you? Are they complete?

A. Yes.

Q. Do they record that she had two aunts that died with ovarian cancer?

A. I recorded that she had a family history of ovarian cancer. I did not record that she had two aunts that died with the disease.

Q. Why not? Why didn't you do a genetic test – BRC1 and BRC2?

A. I recorded that there was a family history of ovarian cancer... that's enough.

Q. Attorney Sanchez: Two years ago, Lori had a abnormal pelvic ultrasound report – describing an enlarged right ovary. Could you show me the radiologist's written report and your notations?

Attorney Reed: Objection. You're assuming there was an abnormal report because there was an enlarged ovary.

Q. Okay. I'll reword my question. Two years ago, Lori had an ultrasound describing an enlarged right ovary. Show me the report and your notations.

A. Dr. Pruitt found the radiologists report suggesting re-examination and close follow-up. His note stated: 'Patient reassured about benign cystic enlargement of the right ovary.'

Q. Did you consider taking a look in the abdomen with a laporascope to check the right ovary at this time? Do a biopsy.

A. No

Q. Did you consider doing a CA-125 blood test to see if it was elevated?

A. No.

Q. Why not?

A. It's not always accurate.

Q. What if it was elevated?

A. I suppose I would be more concerned and aggressive.

Q. What was Lori Karp's CA-125 levels when you found out she had ovarian cancer?

A. It was high.

Q. It was out of sight. Wasn't it? When Lori came in to see you, saying that she was sick with abdominal pain. What was your evaluation?

A. I described my pelvic exam as negative and said that the abdomen was unremarkable.

Q. I noticed that it was a brief note – nothing about bowel sounds, or whether you felt the ovaries. Nothing about doing a vaginal ultrasound, CT Scan or MRI. Please read what you wrote.

A. Negative pelvic and abdominal exam.

Q. How do you account for the fact that three weeks later, Dr. Scott did a rectal exam on Lori and found a grapefruit size mass in the lower right abdomen and a fixed hard pelvis – he also felt a mass in her upper belly?

A. I can't.

Q. Why didn't you remove her ovaries after her childbearing years when she asked you to?

A. She can still get ovarian cancer.

<u>Attorney Sanchez</u>: If you remove the ovaries, her chance of getting

cancer is less than five percent. Isn't that true? She'd be alive

today!... That's all my questions. I reserve the right for further

interrogation of Dr. Pruitt if new evidence presents itself.

The tumor mass in Lori's abdomen continued to grow rapidly inspite of the chemotherapy. Dr. Bern considered a laporoscopy to do a second look inside her belly. She refused. Her pain increased and was unbearable. A morphine drip was placed in her arm so that if she got a severe cramp or pain, she could increase her own dose. Lori didn't want to die... she wanted to see her grandson grow. She was upset with the big bills she was getting for her chemotherapy with no results (six thousand dollars a treatment). She couldn't eat. Her mouth was dry. She was getting bedsores. A decompression tube had to be placed in her stomach to prevent her bowel from filling up like a balloon. The abdominal distension was incredible. Finally, the medical oncologist, Dr. Stone gave up. She couldn't explain why Lori didn't respond. She arranged for Hospice to come in to take care of Lori before she died.

One week before she died, Lori told Dr. Scott that if she had to do it all over again, she wouldn't have taken all that chemotherapy. It didn't work and it was too expensive... over $50,000 for nothing. All it did was make her medical oncologist rich. It made her sick, she lost her hair... had constant nausea and diarrhea and was tired all the time. Her quality of survival was horrible. Lori died eleven months after her diagnosis was made.

The case was all set to go to trial but the defense procrastinated about the settlement. Their argument was that she had an advanced cancer when she was diagnosed and that this was not uncommon with ovarian cancer. The remuneration should be minimal. Dr. Sanchez argued that Lori would be alive if Dr. Pruitt had properly investigated her enlarged right ovary two years earlier. A laproscopic exam and biopsy would have diagnosed the cancer early. He also should have recommended having her ovaries removed.

Finally, the defense realized that the odds of winning were impossible and they settled for over one million dollars. Dr. Pruitt because of the adverse publicity associated with the case at his hospital, resigned from the staff and retired.

The news media, when they read about the settlement, got the court records and used the case for a TV series on ovarian cancer. Maria was paid to comment on the series. She donated the money for basic ovarian cancer research.

When the Medical Supreme Court came into being, she was a unanimous choice to represent the Obstetricians and Gynecologists on the new Medical Supreme Court.

The seven other members selected to sit on the Medical Supreme Court were outstanding members in their respective fields. All had degrees in medicine and law. Family medicine had John Whipple from Hartford Hospital in Hartford, CT. Stacy Goldberg, the Chief of Medicine at Beth Israel Hospital in Boston represented Internal Medicine. Brian Curtis was the Chief of Orthopedics at the Hospital for Special surgery in New York City, and he represented orthopedics. John Hartman from the University of Chicago represented pathology. Victoria Fox from the Mayo Clinic represented psychiatry. Paul Hickman, Chief of Radiology at Washington University in St. Louis, represented radiology and Carolyn Chan, Chief of Anesthesia at Jackson Memorial Hospital in Miami, FL, represented the Anesthesia Society.

Once all the members of the Medical Supreme Court were selected and sworn in by the Chief Justice of the (legal) Supreme Court, Jonathan Oliver Ellsworth, the Medical Supreme Court Justices in secret ballot elected Mark Jackson the First Chief Justice of the Medical Supreme Court. It wasn't long before the Medical Supreme Court was called into its first session.

Two Congressmen went before the Medical Supreme Court. No media or TV was allowed in the courtroom. The Medical Supreme Court functioned perfectly, and the two that went before the Court had a fair trial and discussion of their serious illnesses. The Medical Supreme Court ruled they were disabled and had to be replaced in Congress by an election in their state in three months.

The "old boys" who had controlled Congress for centuries were out because of term limits. You could serve three six-year terms in the Senate and six two-year terms in the House. If you wanted to serve a longer period of time in politics in Washington, D.C., you had to serve in the House first and then in the Senate, but this was not an easy task.

Some members of the legal profession were up in arms because there was no longer lifetime tenure for the Supreme Court Justices. Deans of law schools were furious, because, if their school had a member sitting on the bench, they had easy access to place their law clerks in the Justice's office to gain invaluable experience.

Kelli became the target of many of the lawyers who served in Congress... over fifty percent of its members. They were mad about revisions to the Medical Malpractice gravy train. The trial lawyers could still take part in the majority of the malpractice cases in the District State Courts and Circuit Appellate Courts, but the Medical Supreme Court would have the final jurisdiction over major malpractice cases that were appealed. After all, the judges who were lawyers, determined legal malpractice. Why shouldn't the doctors determine medical malpractice?... the public's wishes prevailed. They knew that there were too many lawyers in Congress. It was an unhealthy mix and not representative of the people.

There was no way Congress could get all the states to have another Constitutional Convention. Kelli had done her job well. The American people knew what was going on, liked what they saw, and what was happening. Unfortunately, more assassination threats were coming into the White House mail and security had to be tightened so nothing would happen to Kelli.

PART TWO

8

KELLI ANNE'S PROM

Mark and the two children had a difficult time adjusting to President Kelli Palmer's busy schedule. Being Vice President was nothing like being President. She was now the most important leader in the world, and there wasn't enough time in the day to accomplish everything that she was called on to do. There was no one who could substitute for her... as former President Truman said, "the buck stops at my door." It seemed as though there was a crisis everyday, and a new confrontation between hostile countries. The rapid dissemination of information around the world with sophisticated methods of communication made the entire world a glass cage now, everybody knew what their neighbor was doing, and whether you liked what they were doing or not, you were also a member of that glass cage too.

The physical and mental demands put on Kelli, would wear out any normal human being... there was no respite that she could use for relaxation. There were times when she didn't see her family for a day or two, and sometimes on overseas trips for as long as a week or ten days. Occasionally, Mark would go with her, but most often he would stay home with the children. Kelli had surrounded herself with what she thought were the leaders in their specialized political fields, and because she had been in the House and Senate, and knew who the best candidates were to do their respective jobs, she was surrounded by intelligent dedicated people. She hand-picked the Secretary of State, John Standish, who was a former Senator from Connecticut, and George Scott for Secretary of Defense from California. He was a former Vice Admiral who was a pilot that she knew and respected. They were great choices quickly approved by the Senate. However, they were all dependent on her for guidance, which she insisted on when making major decisions.

When she traveled overseas, she always tried to call the White House just to talk to Mark and the children. She made a concerted effort to be present for critical events that her two children were involved with.

The oldest child, Kelli Anne, was sixteen now. She was growing up into a beautiful, athletic, young woman with many of her mother's physical characteristics. She was a very independent young lady, and didn't hesitate to give her opinions to anyone on any subject.

She attended private school in Washington, D.C., and was now dating, much to her mother and father's chagrin. She often told off the Secret Service men, and didn't hesitate to tell them to get lost. She often complained to her mother about the agents.

Her brother Paul was into athletics in a big way, and his father attended most of his sporting events. He was not allowed to play football, but he was allowed to play soccer, and because he was big, he played middle fullback on the team. He was one of the school's legitimate stars.

One morning at breakfast, Kelli Anne was mad at her mother and let her know it.

"You're spending less time with Paul, me and Daddy than when you were Vice President, and I don't like it!" she said as she stamped her foot.

"I have to think about all the people in this country, and what's best for them," she replied. "That's why all my time is taken."

"Well, that's not good enough for us."

"Just what do you want?" Kelli asked.

"I have lots of questions. I'm dating now, and I have questions that Daddy can't answer.

"Such as?"

"I like the boy I'm dating now, and he says he wants to get close to me. He wants to kiss me without all those Secret Service agents peeking behind the bushes."

"I don't think there's anything we can do about that. They're out there to protect you… which I think is a good idea for a lot of reasons."

"How old were you when you went out with boys, and started kissing, Mom?"

"I was a tomboy, into sports. It took a while. I don't remember. I hung around with the boys, but didn't get really interested in them in a physical way until I went to the Naval Academy. The rules were rigid there too, about fraternization with the boys as a plebe, during my first year."

"This is a different situation, Mom. I'm only in high school. Kids are more sophisticated now. I'd like some advice that is relevant to right now! Those Secret Service men hanging around are an invasion of my privacy."

"In some ways. I don't like what they do either," said Kelli. "Guarding you against harm is one thing, watching to see what you do and listening to your personal conversations is another. I'll have to think about your problem, Kelli Anne. You should be able to have some semblance of privacy in you own personal life. I'll have to talk to the Secret Service. What is this boy's named that you're dating? It's nothing serious is it?"

"Mom, it can't be serious if it's just getting to the point where he wants to kiss me. That's what I'm complaining about. I can't even get to the first stage of a relationship. I can't get to first base."

"Is he your age or is he older?"

"I'm a junior and he's a senior. He's asked me to go to the Senior Prom. He's a football player, and the class president. He's going to the Air Force Academy when he graduates."

"Sounds okay to me. Sounds like you picked a good one. I'll try to be around to meet him when he comes to pick you up for the prom. Are there anymore details?"

"Four of the guys are renting a limo, and then there's an all night party that we're going to. I hope the Secret Service stays out of my way."

"Well, I guess your father or I will have to talk to the Secret Service about this important event."

"I hope they don't screw it up," said Kelli Anne.

The President was taken aback by the term "screw" used by her daughter, but decided not to comment about it. Her vocabulary had obviously broadened in the last year.

The next week, the President spoke to the Chief of the White House Secret Service about Kelli Anne's complaints concerning privacy, and the upcoming Senior Prom that her daughter was going to.

"Ms. President, your daughter's protection is the most important factor that we have to consider. I'm glad you're talking to me. We'll have to search the area of the dance for bombs, and may have to use a metal detector prior to entrance into the ballroom. You never know what those high school kids are up to."

"Can that be done without making it too obvious?"

"Yes, because we don't want unfriendly people to know that she will be there. We'll talk to the hotel where it's being held. Is it a dinner dance?"

"I'll get the details for you from the school, and also the date of the affair."

"We can do that, Ms. President."

"Is alcohol going to be served?"

"My daughter said that it was, but only for those of legal age. Some of the invited guests can drink."

"That sometimes complicates the shindig."

The day of the special occasion, the prom arrived. Kelli Anne had her hair and nails done. She had bought her own gown for the occasion since her mother couldn't shop with her. A simple, green, snug-fitting, short gown, low in back, and thin spaghetti straps. She had a trim, athletic figure, like her mother, beautiful red hair, sparkling green eyes, and a pretty smile. She also had a personality that was infectious and outgoing. She was almost like a clone, and was almost as tall as her mother. She knew it would be awkward wearing high heels so; she'd have to practice a little with her new shoes before going to the dance.

Kelli Anne was to be picked up at 7:00 P.M. by her date, and so the White House gate had been alerted about the limo.

Her mother and father were anxious to meet the young man that she was going out with, and wanted to have just a few pictures taken by a professional photographer with the two standing together all dressed up in gown and tux.

"You can take a couple of pictures, but that's all Mom. I don't want any big fuss. I might want to go out with this boy again."

"Any other instructions?" asked the President.

"We have an all night party after the dance, at Jack Harrigan's home in Silver Springs. I'll be home after breakfast in the morning."

"Things have certainly changed," the President said to Mark later that evening.

"Well, the Secret Service will be keeping an eye on her, anyway. There's nothing to worry about."

At 6:30 P.M., Kelli Anne came out of the bathroom after taking a shower, applied her make-up, and got dressed. She looked into the full-length mirror, and liked what she saw. She was beginning to realize that she wasn't bad looking, and hoped that someday she'd be a knockout, just like her mother. This would be her first big formal dance, and she was quite excited, and just a little bit apprehensive. She liked the boy she was going out with because he was tall, a six-footer, and had a good physique, handsome facial features, and a good personality. He was easy to talk to, and seemed to be interested in her, and not the fact that she was the President's daughter. His parents were wealthy, which was a given, because in order to be going to the prep school that they went to, you had to be wealthy, although there were a few full scholarship kids there too.

Just before 7:00 P.M., Kelli Anne came out to the living room so that her parents could see what she looked like, all dressed up. The President was amazed at how grown up she looked, and Mark couldn't help but remark, "That young man you're going to the dance with is a real lucky guy! You're beautiful, Kelli Anne, just like your mother."

"Thanks, Dad! I was just a gleam in yours and mom's eye at one time. Here I am, all dressed up for my first prom. I'm very excited."

"I'm sure you're going to have a good time. Be sure that you don't do anything foolish."

At approximately 7:15 P.M., the limo carrying George Price arrived at the front door of the White House. He was greeted by the doorman, and led to the President's family quarters by a Secret Service Agent. The President and Mark were pleasantly surprised when Kelli Anne introduced him to them. He reminded the President of some of the young pilots that she had flown with in the Navy. He was a six-footer, looked like he weighed about 200 lbs, had an athletic physique, a crew cut type of haircut, focused look of intelligence, and a warm smile. She thought that he could easily qualify to be a pilot. He was carrying a small box, which he presented to Kelli Anne.

"I was afraid it might get lost in this big White House," he stated as he presented it to her. "I hope you like it."

Kelli Anne opened the box. It contained three beautiful red roses with baby's breath around it.

"It's beautiful, George. Thank you," she said as she kissed him on the cheek. "Mom will you help me pin it on my dress?"

"Perhaps you should leave it in the box, and have George pin it on when you get to the dance."

"That's a good idea," she replied.

The professional photographer took four pictures and wanted to take more. "That's enough," said Kelli Anne as she went to get a jacket.

She put on a white silk brocade cover-up over her shoulders and said, "George, let's go!"

"Have a good time," said Kelli and Mark as they left.

"I don't know about you, Kelli, but I'm not going to sleep well tonight worrying about our daughter."

"I'll have to admit that I'm going to worry a little bit, too," replied Kelli. "She certainly picked out a handsome guy for her first big prom. I hope they behave."

The Secret Service had set up the security with the hotel in Georgetown. The cocktails, and hors d' oeuvres before dinner were in an adjoining room to the dining room. All the guests would go through a door that had a metal detector. A light would go on – no bells, and an agent would check the guest out.

There was a bar and also regular punch for the non-drinkers, and a spiked punch for the drinkers.

The sit down dinner was set up in the main ballroom, with the dance band, and dance floor there. The main ballroom was adjacent to the back floral gardens.

There were dance cards filled out ahead of time. Most of Kelli Anne's dances were with her date or the other three couples' dates that rode in the limo.

The legal age was eighteen, so Kelli Anne couldn't drink alcoholic beverages, but she had a taste of her boyfriend's drink, which was a watered-down scotch, which she did not like and wanted to spit out. She finally gulped it down.

"Why don't you order a glass of wine, or champagne next time, something sweet, something I might like to share," she told her date.

"No problem," George replied.

He ordered a glass of sparkling French red wine, which Kelli Anne tasted, and kept, for herself. The lights had been dimmed in the ballroom, and the band sounded great. There were quite a few group dances, including the Macarena.

George held her close while they danced, and after a second glass of the forbidden wine, Kelli Anne relaxed, and snuggled up to him. She felt that she was out on the town for the first time and the Secret Service couldn't see anything out on the dance floor because the lights were dimmed way down. Actually, what she didn't know was that there were agents dressed in tuxes, and with young girls for dates, who were also Secret Service Agents, out on the dance floor, too.

Kelli Anne really was enjoying herself. Her date was a perfect gentleman, and he certainly did hold her body close to his. He kissed her on the cheek a few times while they were dancing, and then she decided to kiss him back. She wondered what it would be like to kiss him on his mouth.

"You're a pretty girl, Kelli Anne," said George. "I'd like to get to know you better. I wish you weren't the President's daughter."

"Why?" she asked.

"I'd be kissing you on the mouth, and really getting to know you better."

"Would you behave yourself?" Kelli Anne asked.

"I'd let you control the action," he replied.

"Well, the night is still young. I'm going to give some serious thought to you proposition."

"Good," replied George.

"I don't want you to think of me as the President's daughter. I want you to think of me as anyone of the other girls you've dated. How does that sound?"

"Great! The one trouble with that, however, is the Secret Service. They're all over the place, and it would be hard for us to get to be alone."

"I agree, and I hate it," replied Kelli Anne. "If we're going to get to know each other, we've got to figure out a way to be alone."

"Now you're talking," said George as he pulled Kelli Anne close to him, and planted a kiss on her lips. He held it for a while, and she liked it. When they broke the kiss, the band stopped, and the lights went on, and they walked back to their table.

The Senior Prom was to break up at 1:00 A.M., and then the couples were to go to the private parties. The big party was at the Harrigan Estate high in the hills above Rock Creek Park, near Silver Springs.

Kelli Anne and the group of four couples got into the limo, and soon all four couples were paired up necking en route to the estate. The space was limited in the back of the stretch limo, but there was adequate room for the couples to cuddle up, and get acquainted. There was no hesitating on the part of any of the partners to start kissing each other.

Kelli Anne participated in the get acquainted experience, and enjoyed kissing George, but was turned off somewhat when they were having a breather, when he said, "Kelli Anne, I'm going to have to teach you how to kiss better, how to use your mouth."

"What, you didn't like my kisses?"

"No. You don't understand. Your lips were as soft as a baby's, but the rest of your mouth is suppose to respond to mine."

"I thought it was. If it wasn't, forget it. If you don't like the way I kiss, you can find someone else."

"You don't understand," he replied.

"I guess I don't," replied Kelli Anne. "Either I'm going to have to decide whether I like you enough to let you teach me how to kiss properly or to forget the whole deal."

As she said that, she took his arm off from around her waist, and pushed him away. "I'm going to have to think about what you just said."

The limo finally arrived at the Harrigan Estate. There was a large parking area off to one side. It was obvious that the Harrigan's had had some big parties here in the past. There were at least fifteen limos parked in the lot and numerous Mercedes, Cadillacs, BMW's and Lexus' were also parked there.

When they got into the home, it was obvious that the chaperones were prepared for no hanky-panky. There were numerous parents present to monitor the action. The only drinks that were served were beer, wine and champagne, and only to those that had the proper ID. Punch and soft drinks of any type were also available.

The grounds adjacent to the ballroom had beautiful well-manicured lawns that were like a putting green, and flower gardens that were classically landscaped. For security reasons, there were floodlights all over the place in the gardens, and they were on. If was obviously set up to prevent those males who wanted to disappear in the bushes with their dates.

There was a small seven-piece band in the main ballroom with a D.J., so that most of the recreational exercise took place there. Hors d' oeuvres were available with lots of shrimp, clams, oysters, and lobster morsels. Small roast beef sandwiches would be freshly carved for you.

George knew that he had made a faux pas telling Kelli Anne that she didn't know how to kiss properly. Kelli Anne was one of the prettiest girls in the whole crowd, and he wanted to apologize for the gross error, but didn't know how to do it properly. He finally got up enough nerve.

"Kelli Anne, I want to apologize for that stupid remark I made. I really like you, and want to get to know you better. I hope you will accept my apology."

"I've thought about it too. Maybe I have something to learn about kissing. I'm new at this. We can learn together."

"Good. Then you will go out with me on future dates?"

"Of course! However, in some way we have to figure out a way to get out from under the eyes of the secret Service," replied Kelli Anne.

"Well, we certainly aren't going to be able to get together here at the Harrigan's with all the parents monitoring the activities."

AT THE WHITE HOUSE

The President and Mark had a discussion about their daughter Kelli Anne, after she left for the dance.

"Kelli Anne told me that she's been asking a lot of personal questions that you can't answer. Is that right?"

"Yes. They're teenage girl questions. I don't know how to answer them."

"Such as?"

"When I kissed you first. I told her the truth, that you were twenty-two, and had just graduated from the Naval Academy."

"You're no help," she replied. "I can see some problems developing on the horizon in the future. I think we've got to do something about that. She blasted me about not being available to talk to her, recently. It's time I set aside time to be with her. I've been extremely busy with that Mid East and Asian problem. I need a rest myself. Perhaps we can set up a weeks vacation."

"I think that's a great idea. I'd like to spend more time with my wife, too. When I do see you, you crawl into bed all tired out."

"So, I've got two major family complaints."

"I'd say three. Your son Paul misses you too. He's turning out to be quite a good soccer player. He'd love to see you watch at least one game."

"I'll look at my calendar, and then you can pick a good spot. How's that? I've got a summit meeting in China in two weeks, and then I should be able to take a break. Vice President Hatfield would love to cover me."

THE BISTRO

On the way to the Harrigan's Silver Springs Estate, the couples really got together. They paired off, and there were no stragglers, including Kelli Anne. She quickly learned the art of full mouth kissing. It was a new experience for her, and she wasn't sure she liked it. Some petting was taking place, and there was some haggling about getting into each other's way as the boys strived for a positional advantage with their dates. They split up when they got close to the estate. Most of the girl's dates were legal for alcoholic beverages and it was available if you wanted it. Some of the guys had brought flasks with them to spike the punch. There was also a room set aside for the girls and guys that smoked, and after awhile it had a sweet smell of marijuana. It was obvious that some were not smoking tobacco. The Secret Service however, weren't about to search everyone to find the weed, with the President's daughter in the group.

Kelli Anne was having a great time, and her date was a perfect gentleman, almost. His hands had a tendency to wander about her upper body, and she was not completely displeased by his actions. This was her first big date that she had where she felt somewhat free from the close observations of the Secret Service agents. It made her feel like a free spirit, and there was a little wild streak coming out of her personality. Kelli Anne had two or three glasses of the spiked punch, and she was feeling kind of giddy and completely relaxed.

"Kelli Anne, I want to talk to you about something," said George.

"What's on you mind, besides?"

"As you know, Steve Harrigan, a grandson of the owner of this place, is in our party."

"I know," replied Kelli Anne.

"Well, two of the couples in our limo group, are going to skip away from this party, and go to an all night honky-tonk bistro. Steve Harrigan is one of the guys."

"So. What does that mean?"

"I'd like to join them with you, on the town. We could come back before sun-up, and we wouldn't be missed."

"I think I'd be missed by the Secret Service."

"I don't think so. I don't think that they know where we are right now."

"How are we going to get away to go to this bistro, and how are we going to get there? How far away is it?"

"It's only about fifteen miles away. Steve has stashed a car two blocks away in a friends garage."

"I'd like to go, but I'm afraid something bad might happen."

"We're just going to have a few drinks, do some dancing, and smoke some weed."

"I'll go if you won't smoke weed. You have to promise me!"

"Okay. No weed. It will give us both a chance to get to know each other better. I'm looking forward to that!"

"What time are you planning to leave?"

"In about thirty minutes. We're to meet out in the garden where all the flood lights are."

"There's no way we can leave from there," said Kelli Anne.

Steve, Jack and I have our watches synchronized, you'll see."

There were seven Secret Service agents assigned to monitor the dance, and make sure that Kelli Anne Palmer was not harmed. The agent in charge was Bill Cullop, who had been with the Secret Service for about ten years. They had three sport utility vehicles, and the entrances and exits to the estate had metal detectors that were easily set up. There were large portable high-rise spotlights put up in the outdoor garden.

Two young, attractive female agents were dressed in gowns, and five male agents were dressed in tuxes. The guys had lapel buttons with boutonnieres, and the girls had devices in their floral arrangements. They all carried digital and analog cellular phones.

When the band took a break, the lights were made brighter in the ballroom. "Everything is going too smooth for me," said Bill Cullop, the agent in charge.

Linda Ross, one of the female agents replied, it's better that way than to have trouble. There have been no fights over the girls. No one's got drunk, so far, and only one girl has been vomiting in the john. Another girl was crying because there was a girl wearing a dress just like hers."

"I saw Kelli Anne's boyfriend kissing her on the dance floor," said Bill.

"So what," replied Linda. "He's her date. That's part of the deal."

"I hope that's all of the deal," remarked Cullop. "The night is still young."

"This is an all night affair," replied Linda. "There's a buffet breakfast being served at 7:30 A.M. with all the trimmings. I'm looking forward to that."

"Well, there's a full moon out tonight," said Cullop. "All the kooks come out when there's a full moon. I hate full moons! Something always goes wrong."

"Who's watching the outdoor gardens?"

"Jack Cummings and Tiffany Hart."

"I'm glad they put in those spotlights."

"I'm sure that some of the kids are smoking pot in that smoke room. It sure smells like it."

"Well, you can't blow the whistle. If you do, the President's daughter will be incriminated. If you did, your job would be on the line."

"I haven't seen the President's daughter or her date go into that room."

Kelli Anne's date, George Price kept looking at his watch. It was 12:45 A.M. "Let's go out to the garden," he remarked.

When they got out there, the two other couples were waiting for them. Steve Harrigan reached into his pockets and gave each of the guys a small flashlight he had stashed in the garden.

"Five minutes to countdown," he said. "When it happens, we're all to hold hands and follow me. We'll have to run a little bit. Let's edge over towards the bushes."

At exactly 1:00 A.M., the floodlights in the garden went out. People started screaming, and total bedlam developed.

Bill Cullop in the main ballroom heard the screaming in the garden. Jack Cummings and Tiffany Hart immediately reported that the floodlights had blown.

"That's great," said Cullop. "Christ, where the fuck is the main switch. I hope there are some back-up auxiliary lights. Where's the President's daughter?"

Tiffany Hart responded. "She's out here in the garden."

"We're in deep shit," replied Cullop. "Do we have any portable flashlights? This could be serious." He called to one of the agents in the main ballroom. "Get the band's mike, and tell everyone in the garden to come inside and to enter the main ballroom."

When the floodlights went out in the garden, George grabbed Kelli Anne's hand, and Steve Harrigan, and the three couples ran through the dense gardens. Steve used his flashlight to guide the way once they got away from the house.

They ran until the girls got out of breath, and finally arrived at a garage. The door was open, and inside was a black Jeep sports vehicle.

"Get in the car, and we'll get the hell out of here," said Steve. Within minutes they were driving down the highway, traveling fast, and heading for the bistro.

"Better slow down," hollered George, "or the State Cops will pick us up."

"That's a good idea," he replied, as he cut back on his speed. Within fifteen minutes they were at the bistro. It was off the beaten path, and was aptly named "The One-Eyed Dragon". It was a former skating rink that had been converted into a large dance hall. On top of the roof was a big green dragon with one eye that had bright green puffs of smoke coming out. The building had a large amasite parking area with floodlights all over the place. The dance hall was in a secluded spot set back from the street with large trees surrounding it. There were about a hundred cars parked in the lot. Kelli Anne quickly noted that inside the dance hall it was a multiracial; diffuse ethnic dance hall type of place, with Blacks, Hispanics, Asians and Whites on the dance floor. There was a large circular bar that surrounded the dance floor and there was obviously no carding of the occupants.

The dancers were mostly young college or professional people dressed in whatever you chose to wear. Some were scantly clad, and others wore dressy clothes and gowns – quite a few short dresses with either tank tops or halters were prevalent. It obviously was the "hot spot" for the young jet set crowd who were relaxing, slumming and raising hell. A big twenty-piece band was blasting away with the latest tunes. The bistro was placed ideally out in the woods, so that the neighbors couldn't complain about the noise, cut off time was 4:00 A.M., but sometimes the band passed the hat around for cash and kept playing until 5:00 A.M. There was lots of singles, males and females, seated around the dance floor, and there were more males than females in the crowd. Some of the men seated at the bar were cutting in and dancing with the girls.

"George, I don't want to be cut in on," said Kelli Anne.

"I won't let them," he replied. "You're my date, and my property tonight."

"Good. I hope that you can prevent that from happening. Some of those guys look really big. They look like wrestlers or football players."

Steve Harrigan, evidently knew someone because the mai-tre' d took the three couples to a front table on the dance floor.

"Order anything you want to drink," said Steve.

"I don't want you to drink any heavy stuff, George," said Kelli Anne.

"Just one scotch and water."

"No," replied Kelli Anne. "You can have beer or wine, nothing else, or you can call a cab for me."

"Okay, Kelli. I'll drink the weak stuff and be good."

THE HARRIGAN ESTATE

Back at the ranch, the Harrigan Estate, the Secret Service were in a tizzy. It took more than thirty minutes before the flood-lights came back on and it was established that the President's daughter and her date were missing along with two other couples. Bill Cullop was in a state of panic. He didn't know what to do, and how to react to the problem. He quickly called for back-up Secret Service agents, and told the State Police to put up a roadblock in all directions around the Harrigan Estate. He had to consider that the worst had happened. It could be terrorists who had possibly kidnapped the three couples including the President's daughter.

"Where were you when the lights went out," he asked the two agents assigned to the garden.

"I was out at the deepest part of the garden," replied Tiffany. "And the other agent was closer to the house. The three missing couples were in the middle of the garden."

"God! I hope they're all right. I hope their pulling a prank on us."

"Where's the fourth couple that was with them in the limo?"

"They're here. I've already questioned them. They don't know anything."

"Are you sure?"

"Yes."

"Well, let's see. Where would high school kids go to get away from parentage observation?"

"They'd either go out to raise hell, drink, maybe have sex," said Tiffany.

"You've got to be kidding," said Cullop. "Tell the State Police to check all the motels, night clubs, bistros, etc," he hollered.

"They might even go out in the woods with a blanket," said Tiffany.

"Not the President's daughter," he replied.

"What makes her different than the rest of us?"

"You're right. We don't know whether someone has kidnapped them or whether they're on their own raising hell."

"Should we notify President Palmer that her daughter is missing?"

"Not yet," said Cullop. "We'll have to if we don't find her quickly. Christ, we're in deep shit! We're going to have some big explaining to do."

9 ⚕

OUT ON THE TOWN

Kelli Anne, George, and the other two couples were having a great time at the "One-Eyed Dragon". Kelli Anne got rid of her shoes, and was dancing up a storm, the "Macarena", the 50-s "Jitterbuging", the "Electric Slide", the "Chicken Dance" and all the old and new dances. The dance band was really loud, blasting away and their rhythm was terrific. When the twenty-piece big band took a break, a black D.J. played techno-music. The rotating ceiling psychedelic lights, flashing with all sorts of spotlights, added to the excitement on the dance floor. It was also obvious that some of the dancers had taken either drugs, alcohol, or had the effects of weed in their bloodstream. They were free spirits. Some of the dancer's inhibitions were released, and there was kissing, and fondling taking place on the darker edges of the floor.

Once the music stopped and the lights went on, there was frequent switching of partners. Some knew each other, but others did not. Two or three tried to cut in on George to dance with Kelli Anne, but he refused the transfer, and almost got away with it.

After a "hot number" by the band, Kelli Anne and George had danced up a storm, the music stopped, and a large, Black male, about six foot three inches, weighing about 275 lbs., and all muscle, came up to George and Kelli Anne.

"I'd like to dance with the pretty lady," he said.

"Sorry," said George. "She's taken, and doesn't want to dance with anyone but me."

"That's not the custom at the "One-Eyed Dragon", he replied.

"Custom or no custom, she's not dancing with you," replied George.

"I think the lady's got to refuse," he said, as he reached out to grab Kelli Anne's hand.

"I'll dance with him," said Kelli Anne.

"Good," he replied as he pulled her to him.

"Take a seat for a while," said the Black intruder.

"It's okay," said Kelli Anne. "It's only one dance," she replied as she waved goodbye with her hand to George.

On the dance floor, she found out that the black man's name was Sherman Walters, and he was a former NFL tackle from Pittsburgh. He was an excellent dancer, and was a perfect gentleman. She was pleasantly surprised.

"I have a nickname. I'm called "Bozo" here," he said. "I like to dance, and I noticed that you really know how to dance. You're very pretty, too!"

"Thank you, Bozo," she replied with a smile.

"Why did you quit football?" she asked.

"I had a serious knee injury, and couldn't take the pounding after a while. The opposition kept hitting me in the injured leg."

"That's dirty," replied Kelli Anne.

"Professional football can be dirty," he replied. "There's big bucks involved."

"You seem to know how to dance pretty well," said Kelli Anne.

"It helps me keep my legs in shape," he replied. "It's my form of rehab."

When the music stopped, "Bozo" took her over to the table where George was seated.

"Thank you, young lady. I really enjoyed the dance."

"You're quite welcome," she replied.

Bozo looked at George. "You've got a really nice young lady there. You're a lucky guy," he said.

"I know," replied George.

After he left, George was obviously disturbed that Kelli Anne had danced with him.

"You didn't have to do that," he said, acting mad and looking hurt.

"Would you rather have been flattened on the floor," she said. "Besides he was a perfect gentleman."

"I could have given him a tussle."

"I'm not so sure. He's a retired NFL defensive tackle for the Pittsburgh Steelers."

"I guess you're right. He looked like a big bruiser. Maybe we ought to get out of here."

"I'm not ready to leave. I'm having a great time," she replied. "The other two couples we came with, seem to be having a good time, too!"

Seated at the long bar next to the dance floor were two black and two white skinheads that had taken in all the action with Bozo and Kelli Anne. They had been drinking heavily.

"How come Bozo's dancing with that pretty redhead?" asked one. "He's the bouncer around here, isn't he?"

"Yes. But he likes to dance," said another. "The owner lets him hit the dance floor once in a while."

"He's a has-been football player with no brains," said another. "He should have worn his helmet more."

"I'm not so sure. He may be stupid, but he's tough. He broke up a fistfight last week between three guys over a broad. He flattened them, and I understand one of the guys is still in the hospital with a broken jaw."

"If he did that to me, I'd have used a knife on him, I'd kill him."

"You'd be in jail now," said another, "or waiting for a little electric shock treatment. Do you want to go back?"

"If I was humiliated, and people laughed at me, I'd use that knife."

"You'll end up in the slammer, if you think like that."

"If I could nail that redhead out there, it might be worth it."

"You're talking about rape. That's a major crime."

"I'm going to ask her to dance, and see what happens," he replied.

"I wouldn't do it if I were you."

The white skinhead walked over to Kelli Anne's table, and asked her for a dance.

"I'd like the pleasure of your company on the dance floor," he said as he reached for Kelli Anne's arm.

"She's not dancing," said George.

"If she can dance with Bozo, she can dance with me," he replied.

"Sorry, she's not dancing," said George as he stood up and faced the skinhead.

"You want to go outside, and settle it with our fists?"

"Look, we're here to have a good time, and not have a fight. The lady is taken, and doesn't want to dance with you."

"Oh, so I'm not good enough?"

"That's not it at all. It's a free country, and the lady can choose."

Bozo was in the wings, and saw what was going on. He knew the skinheads. They could be trouble. He walked over to the table.

"Get lost JoJo or you'll have me to deal with."

"I just wanted to dance with the pretty lady, just like you," he replied.

"She's not dancing. She can choose. Leave her alone. Get lost."

Two of the other skinheads laughed.

"JoJo, you're not her type. Bozo is."

JoJo raised his fist, "Shut your mouth."

After the skinheads left, the three couples decided that there might be trouble brewing,

"We ought to leave," said George.

Kelli Anne wanted to stay and was reluctant to leave. She was having such a good time out on the town without any Secret Service agents around.

"They're just a bunch of punks looking for a fight," said Tom, one of the guys in the group.

"We gotta get back to the Harrigan estate in another hour or so while it's still dark," said George. "We might as well go."

AT THE HARRIGAN'S

Bill Cullop, the Secret Service chief in charge, was fit to be tied. He was sweating bullets. There were no leads coming in from the State Police. They didn't know whether Kelli Anne had been kidnapped or the group had taken off on their own. They also didn't know where they were or if they were in a vehicle. Their physical descriptions, and how they were dressed should have made them stand out in a crowd, the men in tuxes and the girls in gowns. Their descriptions were sent out over the police radios. The roadblocks were set up, and were causing all sorts of parking lots on the main highways with the police taking the brunt of verbal abuse. Fortunately, it was late at night, and the traffic wasn't heavy. However, there were lots of trucks out on the highway, and they didn't appreciate being checked. The nightspots and motels were being hit by the State Police, but there were quite a few local nightclubs and bistros in the area. It was a big job and they didn't know where to begin to look.

THE ONE-EYED DRAGON

Back at the One-Eyed Dragon, the skinheads were upset, and were planning revenge. JoJo didn't like being made fun of, and the three other guys were willing to get involved in a rumble. "When they leave, we'll hit them," said Jamey, one of the skinheads.

"We'll take their watches, rings and grab the redhead for some fun later."

"Two of those guys look pretty big," said JoJo. "I got a baseball bat in the back of my car. Besides, there's four of us, and only three of them."

"What about the girls?"

"They'll scream and run," said Jamey. "Maybe, we'll grab all three after we finish off the guys. There'll be one for each of us. One of the girls will have to be shared by two of you."

"Who gets the redhead?" asked Jamey.

"I do," said JoJo.

Inside the dance hall, back at the One-Eyed Dragon, Bozo didn't like what he thought might be developing. Those four skinheads were trouble, one had been in prison, and the other three had been involved in drugs, and had been in a few gang fights. He

decided to mobilize his forces a little bit just in case there was trouble brewing.

There were two other bouncers that worked at the club, and
if necessary they could call the local or State Police. The management didn't like fights because if you called for the police too often,
they'd close down the dance hall. The other two bouncers were
former cops, and were a little bit older, but they knew the ropes.
Norman Shea and Jack Dakin had been in a few skirmishes while
on the force.

"When they leave, we're going to follow them, and make
sure they get off the premises," said Bozo.

George was not happy about what was going on. He had a
bigger responsibility then the rest because Kelli Anne was the President's daughter, and she was his responsibility. He remembers the
President saying, "Take good care of our daughter. Have a good
time, and don't do anything foolish."

They already had done something foolish and they almost
got into a fight with a bunch of thugs. He was getting worried
about their "night on the town". They'd better get out of there and
back to the Harrigan's.

"We've got to get out of here!" said George.

"You're probably right," said Kelli Anne. "That last gang of
skinheads weren't very friendly."

"How do the rest of you feel?"

"We're ready to go. We've got to skip back into that garden
unnoticed, and hope that we weren't missed."

"There were over three hundred people there," said Jim
Muirhead, one of the group. "I'm ready to go, and so is my date. I
sure hope they didn't miss us."

They called for their waiter, and Harrigan picked up the tab
and left a big tip.

The three couples left the dance hall, and walked to where their sport vehicle was parked. Harrigan pressed the button on his keys to light up the vehicle, and as he opened the door, he heard:

"Hey, rich boy, not so fast. You're not going anywhere."

The group turned around, and facing them were the four skinheads. One of them had a baseball bat on his shoulder.

"We want the sports car and the girls, and we won't hurt you guys. Just take off."

"No way," said George. "If you want a fight, make it a fair fight, drop the baseball bat."

"No way," said JoJo. "We're going to knock your brains out with it so you won't be able to recognize us to tell the cops," as he said that, he swung the bat, and almost hit Steve in the head, but he ducked.

George hollered to Kelli Anne, "Run back to the dance hall! Run Kelli!"

"I'm staying to help you fight these goons," she said, as she reached into her purse for her cellular phone. She hit a button that automatically dialed 911. Kelli Anne had a black belt in karate just like her mother.

JoJo started swinging the baseball bat, and missed the head of one of the guys, but got another in the shoulder knocking him to the ground. He screamed in pain, and probably had a fractured arm. He was disabled and knocked out of the fight. Kelli Anne tried to kick one of the guys in the balls, and succeeded as he doubled up and groaned, grasping his crotch.

"I'll kill you for that, you redheaded bitch." As he struggled to get up, she kicked him again in the neck and he rolled over, gasping for air... Kelli's pointed high heels came in handy as the skinhead sat on his butt... holding his neck.

The fists were flying all over the place, and George succeeded in wrenching the baseball bat away from JoJo, and throwing it away. He hit him on the jaw knocking him on his ass. As he got up, he pulled a long switchblade knife out of his pocket.

He started swinging the knife in front of George.

"I'm going to kill you!" he said, as he lunged at George. George leaped to the side to avoid the knife, but fell to the ground.

"I got you now," JoJo said, as he stood over George and raised the knife above his head to plunge it into George's chest.

Suddenly what appeared like a freight train behind JoJo, hit him broadside, and he was thrown up in the air, hit the side of the car and ended up on the top of the roof of one of the parked cars. He gave out a big scream as he was hit, followed by a groan and then silence as he lay on the roof. It was Bozo, who hit him with one of his best tackles. As he was thrown skyward, he probably fractured his ribs when he hit the vehicle. He ended up lying drooped over the roof. He was out of it.

The other three skinheads were no match for the former police bouncers. They were on the ground and handcuffed within minutes.

One of them screamed, "I wasn't going to do anything."

"Yeh, you're a little angel, right?"

Suddenly lights went on all over the place as State Police spotlights lit up the whole parking lot.

"Everybody stay still, and put your hands up over your heads, or you'll be shot," said one of the police officers.

The State Policeman in charge recognized Bozo.

"It looks like you didn't need any help, Bozo," he said. "Whose the guy drooped over the car?"

"It's JoJo, the troublemaker."

"That figures. Where's the President's daughter?"

"Whata ya mean?"

"She dialed 911. Her phone has a special satellite in it. She's here somewhere."

"I'm here," replied Kelli Anne.

Bozo's jaw dropped. "She's the President's daughter?"

"That's right," said the State Trooper. "Half the Secret Service is out looking for this young lady. She's going to have a police escort back to the White House with her friends. Young lady, you're going to have some explaining to do to your mother."

THE DIRGE

It was a sullen group that drove back in the darkness in the State Police cars, to Washington, D.C. The tears, moaning and intermittent silence could have been mistaken for the dirge of a funeral procession. There were three State Police cars with each young couple with their own escort. They weren't talking, and the girls were all sobbing and crying. One of the guys was moaning. He had his arm splinted, and would be going to the hospital.

Kelli Anne had a great time out on the town, but she was a beaten kitten. Her clothes were in disarray; her hair was messed up and her eyes swollen with tears. She knew she was in big trouble. What had planned to be a "good time" dancing at a bistro turned out to be a disaster that could have included the killing of her boyfriend. JoJo had his switchblade knife raised to plunge into George's chest. Luckily, Bozo came to their aid at the right time, and the State Police arrived just a few minutes later. Three of the skinheads would be spending time in the slammer, and JoJo who was ready to stab George would be going back to the penitentiary for a long time.

Cullop, the Chief of the secret service group at the party, was relieved when he received the message that the President's daughter had been found, and was safe. He knew he'd be facing his superiors the next day, and would have some explaining to do, but it was a hell of a lot better than what could have happened. His career could have been on the line if something happened to the President's daughter.

Sitting in the back of the State Police's car, Kelli Anne had the shivers, and fought the urge to cry. George was quiet sitting next to her, but his complexion was as white as a sheet, as he contemplated meeting Kelli Anne's parents. What could he say? What should he say? He felt like crying himself. Brave men don't cry but he didn't feel brave right now. The President's daughter could have been hauled off, and stabbed or raped, and that skinhead could have killed him with the switchblade. In retrospect, his judgment was that of an idiot that should be horse whipped, and he knew it. He felt his heart pounding from the intense anxiety, and stress that he had just been through. He had the urge to say something to Kelli Anne, who was shaking like a leaf trying to hold a sob back, sitting next to him. He finally blurted out, "I'm sorry."

Kelli Anne didn't respond. She took his hand and then burst into tears, crying out of control. Finally, she got hold of herself and meekly said, "It's not your fault. I wanted to do it just as much as you did. I was having such a good time until those skinheads butted in."

"I guess this will be the end of our brief romance," he said.

"We'll have to cool it for awhile. I don't know how my parents are going to react."

When the State Police motorcade got back to the White House, all of the three couple's parents were waiting for them in the President's family quarters. The confrontation was not a happy one.

After a brief hugging session, the President remarked, "Thank God, you're all safe!"

Kelli Anne gained her composure, faced her mother and spoke up for the group. "It's all my fault," she said. "I encouraged the boys to do what we did. I was fed up with the Secret Service watching me like a monkey in the zoo. I wanted a 'night out on the town' without the Secret Service peeping behind the bushes. To put all your minds at rest, we drank a little wine, did a lot of dancing, and were having a good time until some skinhead goons broke into our party. They were looking for a fight. They were going to beat up the guys, and haul us off into the woods. The boys fought for our lives, and their own. A nice black man named Bozo saved us. He was a former Pittsburgh Steelers tackle. I'm sorry, Mom and Dad for what we did. I was so frustrated. I'll stop there and like my mother says in the press conferences, "I'll take one question."

"How could you do that?" asked the President.

"I think I answered that question, Mom", as she started to cry and went into her parent's arms. "I don't want to discuss it anymore."

One week later, there was an article in the Washington papers describing in detail the escapade that the President's daughter had experienced. Reporters had interviewed the management of the One-Eyed Dragon, and also got permission to interview the skinheads. Bozo wasn't talking. His only comment was that he was doing his job, doing what he was paid to do. When all the details of the assault got out, he was considered a hero, and was invited to come to the White House by the President. She personally thanked him.

After things calmed down, the President and her husband had a long talk about how the situation should be handled.

"I've got to put some time away from my busy schedule each week to spend with my family. I just have to do it! I've got to spend some time trying to answer my daughter's questions. I don't blame Kelli Anne for what she did. She's a lot like her mother. I wasn't a little angel growing up, but there was one major difference. I didn't grow up in the White House. I know what she was doing. She was rebelling about growing up in the White House. She wanted to have a normal transition into adulthood like most teenagers do, if you can call it that. Unfortunately, that can't happen."

The bistro, the One-Eyed Dragon was not shut down by the State Police. If anything, their business increased because the President's daughter had danced there. Bozo was given a bigger salary, and the management added two more bouncers to the staff.

If was fashionable to go to the One-Eyed Dragon now by the jet set, because of the publicity generated by the President's daughter. The management made some major changes. Better bands were playing there now, and the rules were stricter. No drugs or marijuana on the premises… Although, some of the dancers looked like they were under the influence. A D.J. played hip-hop and electronic music when the big band took a break. There were more lights on, too. Kelli Anne was allowed to go back to the One-Eyed Dragon with George, but the security was tight as a drum. She wanted to pay back Bozo for what he had done to save their lives. In fact, she had another dance with Bozo, and the photographers were allowed to take pictures. The pictures appeared in the Washington papers and the One-Eyed Dragon had sell-out crowds for awhile. It helped to make Bozo a celebrity, and not a has-been football player. He got invited to some talk shows and was paid handsomely for his appearances.

10

THE AFTERMATH

Kelli sat down with her daughter and had a heart-to-heart talk about the One-Eyed-Dragon fiasco. She pointed out that she was not an ordinary child and as long as her mother occupied the chair of the Presidency, she would be a target for terrorists, kooky citizens or other lunatic fringe groups.

"Mom, this was my first big date and I wanted to fit in with the crowd."

"I know and I understand," replied her mother. "You're going to find out that the hardest thing to do in life, is to say "no" and to stick by it. You and your escort were fortunate that you weren't kidnapped, raped and even killed by those goons."

"I realize that, Mom, and I'm really sorry."

"I blame myself and my job," said Kelli. "Not you. I know that I haven't been a good mother in this crucial time in your life. I promise to do better and spend more time with you."

"It won't happen again," replied her daughter.

There were heavy tears in both their eyes as they sobbed and came together and hugged each other.

Getting together was easier said than done. Kelli was the leader of the strongest and greatest nation in the world. There wasn't enough time in the day to address all the world's problems. The world was a vast globe with different time zones, and it wasn't unusual for Kelli to be awakened in the middle of the night by a security agent to discuss problems with Kings, Presidents, Prime Ministers and even Dictators.

Not all had attained their leadership role by a vote of the electorate. Some were anointed, others appointed, and still others replaced assassinated rivals. There were no specific qualifications for the job. Military coups were not uncommon and sometimes the person replaced had an unpleasant demise. Terrorist activity was still rampant around the world and the threat of a missile attack had escalated because of the increased number of countries with nuclear missile capability. China was selling missiles to anyone who wanted them and had the money. If a large city was hit by a missile or the seat of government successfully attacked, the destruction created or the response to that type of activity could create a total holocaust for the world.

A defensive missile shield, after considerable pro and con arguments in the U.S. Congress was constructed. It was extremely expensive and the military leaders were not confident that it would control a coordinated attack by one or more assailants. A defensive missile was like trying to hit a bullet coming at you with a bullet and then hope that what you were hitting was not a decoy.

Newer methods of defensive missile shields were being developed... a gatling-gun type launching pad with multiple defensive missiles that can be fired at once. When they get into the atmosphere, they explode like Fourth of July fireworks that burst into hundreds of stars, each star capable of destroying incoming missiles or decoys...you're not relying on a bullet hitting a bullet.

When it became time to construct the defensive sites in various locations, no one wanted them -- they would be the first targets of any possible global war. A compromise was reached in Alaska by choosing St. Lawrence Island, one of the larger Aleutian Islands off the Alaskan Peninsula. Kodiak Island was considered but it was too close to the Alaskan mainland and created too much public opposition. Guam and Hawaii in the Pacific were also considered but were put on the back burner for future sites.

The deployment of fleet carrier groups with aircraft carriers, Aegis cruisers and nuclear submarines were less controversial and less vulnerable than fixed missile defensive stations. The fleet had the capability of movement and was able to surveil and manage large battle spaces. The day-to-day presence of the fleet around the world, left few hot spots far from the Navy's reach, and kept possible conflicts forward, far away from the states. There were also new undisclosed Star-War defenses.

Because of what had happened with Kelli Anne, the President designated Friday night as "family night" when she was in town. That meant that spending time with her family had the top priority on Friday. The Secret Service was made aware of this, so it had to be a big emergency to interrupt the family gathering. One member would select the menu for the dinner -- it could be pizza, hot dogs and beans, McDonald's hamburgers or a grilled chicken family meal. Occasionally, a full-course gourmet meal would be served if they had outside guests.

Kelli looked forward to her Friday night meal with the family. It didn't always run smoothly without interruptions, but many times it was fun. They would play cards and games including Monopoly or Scrabble.

One night while playing Monopoly, she was abruptly interrupted by the Secret Service. "You're wanted in the Security Room, Ms. President."

Kelli left and walked with the agent to the elevator that descended to the security room. Seated around a large boardroom table were her security advisors and senior members of the military. Her Secretary of Defense, George Scott, National Security Advisor, William Sharp and members of the Joint Chiefs of Staff were also present.

The look on their faces indicated that there was trouble brewing and that it was serious. Kelli looked up at the global screen which showed some lighted areas. She sat down slowly in her chair at the head of the table and looked at George Scott, her Secretary of Defense.

"What's up, George?"

"We've picked up some interesting satellite surveillance pictures, Ms. President."

"Put them on the screen," replied Kelli.

"These satellite pictures show at least four Russian subs on the surface in the Bering Strait, the sea between Russia and Alaska. If you watch closely, they will disappear just before they reach the Russian coastline."

"What does this mean?"

"One of our attack subs has been tracking the Russian subs and has reported that they have a large underwater submarine base built into the coastline. The base is less than a few hundred miles from our Alaskan missile defensive unit at St. Lawrence Island."

"That's interesting. Why is this so important?"

"We have more to show you," replied Scott. "Put the next satellite film on. This global tracking satellite shows a large Chinese landing force, forming on land across from Taiwan, and a large Chinese naval force heading toward the Philippine Sea area."

"I thought that China was going to peacefully try to acquire Taiwan and what's China doing in the Philippine Sea?"

"That's a good question," replied Scott. "Taiwan knows about the force. They have announced that they will fight."

"How can they fight such a large Chinese armada? Why would China want to destroy one of the best producing small countries in the world?" remarked Kelli.

"That's another good question," replied Scott. "Our intelligence units tell us that Taiwan has gotten their hands on some sophisticated defensive missiles."

"Where could they get defensive missiles?"

"They're American missiles or excellent copies. They got them in the "black market". They may have gotten some missiles from the Middle East."

"Now I've heard everything," replied Kelli. "I can't believe it."

"Not quite," said the Defense Secretary. "Our spies in Beijing tell us that the head of the Russian Army and some of his staff met with the Chinese military staff last week. They could be planning a coordinated military operation."

"It looks like we do have big trouble. Well, what are we doing to respond?"

"We have two of our latest carrier groups off Taiwan and one in the Philippine Sea area, and have increased our nuclear attack subs up in Alaska."

"Anything else?"

"Yes. We have two N.S.C.'s off the coast of China and another two off the Japanese coast heading for the Yokasuka Naval Base in Tokyo."

"What are N.S.C.'s?" asked Kelli.

"They're our latest Navy weapon. Star Wars satellites can't pick them up. they're called, Nuclear Submarine Carriers. I'll project one of them on the screen for you."

"There's no conning tower on that flat based ship," replied Kelli.

"That's right. It can raise or lower one when it's below or above the surface."

"It looks like a skateboard or a knife cutting through the water."

"That's right. In a battle it makes it harder to hit and harder to find. It's the fastest ship in the world. It has two decks, a flat landing area on the top and a flat hangar deck for the planes, crew and armament. Below that is the nuclear propulsion unit."

"What does it do?"

"In contrast to the large surface carriers, the N.S.C.'s avoid the vulnerability of a surface vessel and also avoids detection by the global satellites."

"It can launch manned or unmanned stealth aircraft or missiles. It can fire high-energy laser weapons and bounce them off a system of satellites and strike a target anywhere around the world. It also has four detachable small submarines eighty feet long, that fit on the side of the N.S.C.'s... two in front and two in back. Their engines can be started up for added power. They can be released from the N.S.C. in a fight or retrieved, and they carry special armor-piercing nuclear torpedoes. The small subs also act as a safety device, an escape mechanism, if the main vessel is injured or sunk. They attach to the large sub. It's an ultimate stealth weapon that can go beneath the surface of the water, or on the surface to launch aircraft, or retrieve aircraft and retrieve small submarines."

"All I can say is, Wow! Do our enemies know we have the N.S.C.'s?"

"We don't know. We don't believe that they have seen the flight components of this ship. The aircraft can automatically be landed on the top surface of the submarine."

"That's an amazing new weapon," said Kelli. "Someone in the Navy ought to get a medal for thinking that one up. Is there anything else?"

"We have reliable information that you will soon be presented with the threat that China is going to militarily take over Taiwan or invade the Philippines. Also, that Russia with their ICBM's will announce that they will support the takeover. Russia is deploying their submarines in areas that may give them an advantage against our defensive shield if there is a shoot-out."

"How do you know this?"

"We have double agents in China that have given us this information."

"Is that correct?" Kelli asked her C.I.A. Intelligence Chief, Deckers.

"Yes. We have been in communication with them."

"How do we know they're telling the truth?"

"We don't. If they're lying, there are ways to deal with them."

"In other words, we have two major powers conspiring to get their way."

"That's right!"

"What's in it for Russia?"

"We don't know. There's a trade-off somewhere."

"How are we going to avoid this potential Armageddon?" she asked her National Security Advisor, Bill Sharp.

"We have to decide exactly what our position is concerning Taiwan and the Philippines and announce it boldly," said Sharp.

"Are we willing to go to war over a tiny island off the coast of China?"

"Does China realize the consequences if we fight her?"

"Do we both understand the consequences?" said John Standish, the Secretary of State.

"Will there be anything left to fight for?"

"I suggest a subtle sledgehammer," said the Secretary of Defense, Scott.

"What might that be?" Kelli asked.

"Unleash the wrappings around the Navy's new N.S.C.'s. That'll scare the shit out of them. We'll probably hear the uproar all the way back here in Washington."

"Won't that just increase the armament race?" volunteered Standish.

"What do you think they're doing -- amassing their troops for the invasion off the coast of China or the Philippines, and Russia putting nuclear subs next to one of our missile defensive shields? They're not just playing games, they're preparing for war," replied Scott.

"How many of the N.S.C.'s do we have?" asked Kelli.

"We have seven completed and three more under construction. All we need to do is show them one submarine carrier and I predict that we've checkmated their operation."

"Why?"

"Because they don't have anything to counteract our nuclear submarine carriers. Their satellites won't know where they are until we fire at them. It's a no-win situation for them. The only problem we have is that the international press and the major countries, are going to scream bloody murder when we announce our new weapon."

"I'll handle that," replied Kelli. "Hopefully, it will do the trick and prevent a nuclear war." Kelli looked at the group seated around the table. She hesitated and then pounded her fist down on the table. "Gentlemen, I've heard all I need to know to make a decision. Let's go for it! Prepare a release for the press as soon as possible. Tomorrow I'll have a press conference."

When the news release of the N.S.C.'s (Nuclear Submarine Carrier) came out, there was an uproar heard around the world. The Secretary General of the United Nations was asked to immediately call a meeting of the Security Council for the purpose of embarrassing the U.S. with a prolonged diatribe of condemnation by the major powers. Russia and China were particularly disturbed because the N.S.C. was a new weapon that they would have to deal with.

PRESIDENTIAL PRESS CONFERENCE
THE WHITE HOUSE

The Chairman of the Joint Chiefs of Staff, the Secretary of Defense, the Secretary of the Navy and the head of the National Security Council were all in attendance when President Palmer entered the White House Press room the next day. All the journalists, newspaper editors and other media personnel stood up.

When Kelli got to the podium, she remarked:

"Please be seated. Members of the press and invited guests, during this past week, our defense satellite systems picked up some unusual military activities that suggested that our country's missile defense units might be tested in the near future. I met with our National Security Advisor, our Secretary of Defense and Secretary of the Navy and the Joint Chiefs of Staff, and decided to release information about a new weapon that our government has developed -- the Nuclear Submarine Carrier. It is now operational and could be a deterrent to aggressive potential military activity. I have called this Press Conference to inform the world that this weapon will never be used as a preemptive weapon against any nation. However, we will not hesitate to use it in defense of our country or to prevent other nations who may provoke an unwarranted attack that might destroy the world. I have asked the Secretary of Defense and the Secretary of the Navy to come to this press conference to demonstrate this new weapon and reveal the problem that we faced."

The Secretary of Defense stood up and a large screen was released from the ceiling and a projector was used to show copies of the satellite photos of Russian Submarines in the Bering Sea. He also showed photos of the buildup of Chinese forces off the coast of Taiwan and the Philippines.

"As the press knows, our government supports any Democratic Government and in particular Taiwan, if it wishes to remain Democratic," said Kelli. *"However, if Taiwan votes in a fair election that they wish to become a member of the Chinese Government, we will also accept that. We will not let any aggressor, force their form of government on anyone. Our Secretary of the Navy will now show you some still pictures and video films of one of our new nuclear submarine carriers. We will not go into any details about size, speed, weaponry, or other military capabilities. However, I assure you that it is awesome. The Secretary of Defense and the Secretary of the Navy will take questions from the press upon completion of the video."*

The video showed a long, flat ship with a conning tower on one side that could be raised or lowered. It also showed the ship submerging and breaking through the surface and launching aircraft and landing planes on its flight deck. It created a formidable sight of military might. When the video was finished, all the hands of the journalists in the room were raised.

Kelli pointed to Mabel Ritzmeyer of the Washington Press Corps.

"Ms. President, how could this massive new type of ship be developed without the other nations not knowing about it?"

"We don't know that they don't know about it. They probably know or suspect that something new was happening but they didn't know exactly what it was, until today."

"How many of these N.S.C.'s do we have?"

"Several," replied Kelli, "and they are operational."

"How many?"

"That information is confidential," interrupted the Secretary of Defense.

Kurt Whalen of the Chicago Sun Times raised his hand. "What if China tries to put troops on Taiwan?"

"The Congress and myself have made a commitment which was clearly stated by the Secretary of Defense," replied Kelli.

"Is Russia thinking about invading Alaska?" asked Shirley Jones of the San Francisco Chronicle.

"I don't think so, but they would like to because of its oil reserves and other riches. However, if they value their own country, they'd better not provoke an attack on one of our states."

"You stated that the N.S.C. is in service at the present time. Will the public be able to board and see one of these vessels in the near future?"

"Only naval personnel from the ship will be allowed aboard. However, in order to verify that we have this new type of vessel, one N.S.C. will be in the Yokasuka Naval Base outside of Tokyo tomorrow. The ship will be allowed to be seen from a dis-

tance and a few invited foreign media will be allowed to board her, including the Chinese and Russians."

"What if Russia or China does fire an ICBM at us, even after seeing the N.S.C.'s?" asked Nick Volpe of the Washington Post.

"Our spy satellites will pick up their location and we will annialate that area completely... I don't think they're that stupid!"

"What did this N.S.C. ship cost?" asked Bill Collins from the St. Louis Post.

"It was expensive but well worth it for what it does," replied Kelli. *"It prevents war!"*

The response to the President's Press Conference was predictable or unpredictable depending on which side you were on. The doves were furious about the new weapons, the hawks thought it was terrific. The media wanted more information and interviews. The major countries involved wanted to talk to President Palmer, immediately. In fact, the Russian Ambassador in Washington D.C. asked for a meeting with the President and this was granted. He came to the White House and was obviously disturbed when she offered her hand.

"Why did you show those photos of our new sub base in the Bering Sea?"

"Because I wanted the world to know what you were up to."

"You made us look like we were the villains."

"Well, aren't you?"

"No," he replied.

"We would not have had to develop those new weapons, if we could trust you."

"You will regret this," he remarked.

"I don't think so, Mr. Ambassador. We want your country to think twice or maybe three times before you make a big mistake that could start a war. You were the aggressor, Mr. Ambassador!"

"You should apologize publicly," he said.

"I'd give it to you, if we had done something wrong. But we didn't. You're excused," she curtly remarked and then turned and walked away.

The Chinese Ambassador met with Kelli the next day.

"Ms. President, our country was only assembling forces to demonstrate our military might to the Taiwanese people. They are not cooperating in letting us take over and occupy their country."

"The satellite photos speak for themselves, Mr. Ambassador. "That's the largest force that China has assembled in one place. What was your Navy doing off the Philippines?"

"We were in the open ocean like your Navy?"

"Well, you certainly fooled me and our military."

"Our country will not wait forever for Taiwan to join us," he replied.

"Taiwan has valuable resources and their people are very industrious. Right now, they want to be Democratic and we will support them," replied Kelli.

"This could lead to war," he replied.

"I don't think so. The island and its people would be destroyed in any major conflict and then it would be worthless."

"Would your country be willing to risk a major conflict over such a small island?"

"The American people are a strong-willed Democracy," replied Kelli. "We have fought in the past for our freedom and for the freedom of other nations. We cherish it. Don't test our will to fight."

The world's media was supportive of what President Palmer had done, particularly the small countries that were struggling to maintain their own independence. Kelli finally agreed to a summit meeting but insisted that major topics and issues be discussed. She was opposed to photo-ops to consolidate legacies for the history books. Geneva, Switzerland was chosen for the summit site.

After three weeks of frustrating scripted meetings, a document was signed by the participating members. It was a fancy piece of parchment paper with a seal on it that many felt was meaningless but might satisfy the media who were the main beneficiaries.

When Kelli flew back from Geneva, Switzerland, she was met at Dulles International Airport by her husband and two children.

When they got back to the White House, she had a stiff drink and remarked, "I never heard so much bull and hogwash presented to high level officials as I did in Geneva. We accomplished nothing! I had to listen because I was constantly asked irrelevent questions by the international press. There was so little important content expressed that it was difficult for me to give intelligent answers."

"You're saying that it was a waste of time?"

"That's right! Except I did accomplish something when I met individually with the President of China and the President of Russia. We all agreed on one thing and that was that we were all sitting on a power-keg of terrorist activity and nuclear annihilation."

Kelli Anne, the daughter spoke up. "Mom, you promised us that you would go on vacation with us when you got back. Are you going to keep your promise?"

"Yes. I need to recharge my batteries. I'll call the Secret Service and have them set up a vacation for us in Hawaii. Perhaps we can go to the island of Maui where your Dad and I spent some time before we were married."

"I'll arrange the vacation," said Mark. "I'll talk to the Secret Service."

PART THREE

11 ⚕

MEDICAL SUPREME COURT
WASHINGTON, D.C.

The vacation would have to wait. There was a lot of activity taking place on the domestic scene. The big corporations were mad about term limits. It was much more difficult for them to control the rising upstarts that were being elected to replace the Congressmen who no longer qualified to participate in the elections... there were quite a few. The health of the candidates was also raising a ruckus. If someone had a major catastrophic illness, they were out. Medical records of the candidates, were now an open book and the majority of the populace wanted young, vigorous people to represent them. Some Congressmen tried to hide serious medical defects.

The trial lawyers weren't happy about the Medical Supreme Court having the final jurisdiction over major malpractice cases. They were lobbying Congress to draw up a new amendment to abolish the Medical Supreme Court. Some members in Congress listened to their arguments but the lawyers were unable to mobilize enough support.

When the Supreme Court was made part of the Constitution in the Judiciary Act of 1789, they had very little to do because it was an appeals court and the principal source of the appeals had to come from the lower federal courts, the district and appellate courts. It looked like that might happen to the Medical Supreme Court because the trial lawyers did not want to appeal medical malpractice cases heard at a district or appellate court... the result was taken out of their hands. However, the law was similar for both Supreme Courts in accepting to hear cases. Review of lower court decisions would take place only upon agreement of the Court to hear the case. The Parties involved filed briefs supporting their positions and after the Supreme Courts review, it would be accepted or rejected. If rejected, the lower court position would prevail. If the justices, after a study of the briefs of the attorneys who represent the litigants, decide to review the case, they hear arguments and the court votes and a majority vote determines the outcome.

Sam Johnston
Plaintiff
vs
John Hepburn, M.D.
Defendant

It didn't take long for hotly contested malpractice cases to work their way through the District and Appellate Court system to the Medical Supreme Court. The jury system was having difficulties in reaching a just and honest decision in complicated medical malpractice cases. The jury, which is made up of laymen, had insufficient intellectual scientific training or knowledge to sort out what was right or wrong, even if the lawyers tried to educate them. The lawyers didn't understand the cases themselves, let alone, try to teach the jury. When they did reach a decision, it was often wrong and the case had to be decided at a higher court level. The judge and the jurors' inability to understand complex medical information, or statistics, or cause and effect relationships, interfered with the court reaching a just decision. They were unable to resolve complex questions of causality. The Medical Supreme Court which was made up entirely of Doctors of Medicine with JD Law School degrees were better able to understand the complex medical cases and make a just legal decision.

The legal methodology of the Medical Supreme Court was set up similar to the regular Supreme Court, in that each justice had law clerks that helped review the cases presented before the court. They helped in reviewing the briefs. There was a big difference in the law clerks, however. The law clerks that worked for the Medical Supreme Court all had double degrees – medical and law. Usually, the Medical Supreme Court Justices and one of his law clerks would review the prospective case prior to presentation before the court. The law clerks were selected from the top law schools in the country.

A major malpractice case with national visibility soon reached the Medical Supreme Court in Washington, D.C. The media became involved when two of the Senators in Congress were diagnosed with prostate cancer and the information had to be disclosed. One of the Senators from Virginia was found to have an advanced prostate cancer and would have to leave the Senate. Senator Sam Johnston was upset because his political career would be over, and his life expectancy considerably shortened. He contacted the law firm of Cockran, Stevens, Packard and Sussman in Washington, D.C., to institute a medical malpractice suit against Dr. John Hepburn, a prominent Urologist in Richmond, Virginia. Dr. Hepburn retained the services of Henderson, Roberts, Cole and Jackson to defend him.

The D.C. law firm representing Senator Sam Johnston, had difficulty getting a top Urologist in Virginia to testify against Dr. Hepburn. They finally got a Surgical Oncologist from out of state, who had trained at Memorial Sloan-Kettering Hospital in New York City to take the job as an expert witness. It was Dr. Jack Dixon, who was from New England.

The trial took place in the Superior Court of Richmond and it was obvious that the local jury did not want to punish their respected local Urologist. They ended up with a "hung jury" and the case was appealed to the Medical Supreme Court.

MEDICAL SUPREME COURT
Washington, D.C.

Sam Johnston
vs.
John Hepburn, M.D.

The Medical Supreme Court building was a beautiful new structure made out of grey granite and marble with large columns in front. The chambers where the court sat had an aura of majesty, beauty and solemnity. Behind the bench, etched out of the black marble walls, in large gold print, was the Hippocratic Oath. In the center was a large vertical caduceus in gold, with the emblematic staff and two serpents coiled around it... a symbol of the medical profession. On both sides of the caduceus were two large scales in gold indicating the scales of justice.

The floors were covered with plush forest green rugs. Stretching across the courtroom in the front was the bench at which the nine justices sat. The courtroom was divided by the traditional "bar" which was made of black walnut wood and ornate brass, separating that part of the room reserved for lawyers admitted to practice before the Medical Supreme Court and the general public. There were two sets of counsel tables within the bar... in the back were two hundred upholstered seats of green velvet for the admitted spectators – tickets only. All entrances had police marshals and metal detection devices.

The Marshall of the court, in his resplendent uniform, sitting at a desk to the right of the big bench where the nine justices would be seated, rose, pounded his gavel and called out:

"All rise!"

The nine justices dressed in long black robes with green and gold slashes on their upper arms, indicating that they were doctors and lawyers, marched in and stood behind their chairs.

The Marshall intoned his familiar words:

"Oyez, oyez, oyez, the Honorable, the Chief Justice and Associate Justices of the Medical Supreme Court of the United States. All persons having business before this honorable court are admonished to draw nigh and give their attention, for the court is now sitting. God save the United States and this honorable court."

Chief Justice Mark Jackson, pounded his gavel down, the Justices were seated and the trial began. He announced:

"This court will now consider arguments in the case of Sam Johnston versus John Hepburn, M.D...

I would like to remind the lawyers participating in this case, that the Medical Supreme Court Justices have all reviewed the briefs by your law firms and discovery portions of this case (depositions) from the previous trial at the Superior District Court in Richmond, Virginia. You have one hour to present your arguments."

CASE HISTORY

Presented by: Donald Parker, Esq.
For Sam Johnston
The Plaintiff

"Your Honor, I will present a brief history of the case and then give the reasons why we feel malpractice has taken place:

Sam Johnston, the plaintiff, developed kidney stones when he was twenty-five years old and consulted John Hepburn, a Urologist in Richmond, Virginia. He was treated successfully and was seen intermittently by the Urology group. When he became a Senator, he was occasionally seen in Washington, D.C. at the University Hospital. Four years ago, at the age of forty-eight, he was treated for acute urinary retention by John Hepburn. He had a rectal examination, his prostate was tender, the bladder was drained, and diagnosis was an infection of the prostate (prostitis). He received three different antibiotics over the course of one-and-a-half years and his prostate was frequently massaged rectally to remove the pus.

He continued to have urgency, so a cystoscopy (look inside the bladder) was done and his diagnosis was changed to benign prostatic hypertrophy due to enlargement of his gland to double its size. He was given a medication (Hydrin) to increase his urinary flow.

He continued to have difficulty in passing his water and saw Dr. Hepburn, who did a rectal digital exam of his prostate on numerous occasions. Two years later, he was given Proscar to treat his BPH, to try to shrink it's size. Repeated rectal exams were done but no blood studies. Six months later, at the age of fifty-two, while he was speaking to a large political gathering at the Century Hotel in Los Angeles, he suddenly got sweaty and collapsed at the podium.

He was immediately taken to the E.R. at UCLA Hospital and was catheterized for acute urinary retention. A rectal exam by the E.R. doctor revealed a large hard prostate that had grown outside the capsule to involve the surrounding seminal vesicles… suspicious for prostate cancer. A blood P.S.A. test was done which was very high (1600), and rectal ultrasound with biopsy revealed diffuse involvement of the prostate with cancer. A CAT scan and MRI of the pelvis revealed that his cancer had spread to the pelvic and abdominal lymph glands and to his bones.

He transferred his care to Dr. George Ewing, Chief of Urology at the University Hospital, in Washington, D.C., where a bilateral orchidectomy (removal of his testicles) was done and his P.S.A. levels (Prostatic Stimulating Protein) fell to 6.5. Dr. Ewing felt that Senator Johnston's prognosis was poor.

"Your Honor, it is our opinion that there was a delay in diagnosis. The urologist did multiple inaccurate rectal prostate examinations and massage. A blood PSA test was not done until he had an advanced cancer of the prostate four years after first being seen. We also believe that a cystoscopy should have been done earlier, with a transrectal ultrasound and biopsy… Our client is now in the most advanced stage of prostate cancer (D stage) with just a short time to live.

"We would also like to state for the record, Your Honor, that our law firm had difficulty in obtaining a urologist to testify against Dr. Hepburn in Virginia. We searched around the country and finally obtained the services of a cancer specialist from New England to be our expert witness, Dr. Jack Dixon. We would like his deposition and testimony in Richmond, Virginia be made part of this Supreme Court's record."

Chief Justice Jackson, "I believe we have that already. If not, it is so granted."

GENERAL COURT OF JUSTICE
SUPERIOR COURT DIVISION
Richmond
Virginia

Sam Johnston
Plaintiff
vs.
John Hepburn, M.D.
Defendant

DEPOSITION OF JACK DIXON, M.D.

A P P E A R A N C E S :

For the Plaintiff
Cockran, Stevens, Packard and Sussman
Washington, D.C.
By: Donald Packard, Esq.

For the Defendant
Henderson, Roberts, Cole and Jackson
Richmond, Virginia
By: David Kirk, Esq.

Sharon Johnson Registered Legal Professional Transcriber

Deposition took place in the offices of:

Henderson, Roberts, Cole and Jackson
1309 Constitution Place

Richmond, Virginia

JACK DIXON, M.D., having first been duly sworn, deposed and testified as follows:

DIRECT EXAMINATION

BY MR. DAVID KIRK, Esq.:

Q. Please, Doctor, tell me your full name.

A. Jack Dixon, M.D.

Q. Dr. Dixon, my name is David Kirk. I'm an attorney practicing in Richmond, Virginia. My client, in a lawsuit which is pending in Richmond, Virginia, is Dr. John Hepburn. He is a Urologist that has practiced in Richmond for a number of years. The case that we're involved with is a medical malpractice case. We are here today to take your deposition because you are one of a number of physicians who has been designated on behalf of the plaintiff, Sam Johnston, as a potential expert witness that may be called upon at the trial of this case to provide expert medical testimony adverse to my client, Dr. Hepburn. Do you understand that you have been so designated by the plaintiffs?

A. Yes, I do.

Q. I'm going to ask you some questions about any opinions that you might have today, Dr. Dixon. Medical records generally speak for themselves, so I'm not going to spend a lot of your time and my time reviewing them. I would appreciate it if you could let me know if you do not understand any question that I ask, because I would like to be certain that you are answering the question as it's posed, okay?"

A. Right.

Q. Did you bring your curriculum vitae?

A. Yes.

Q. May I have it? Mark this as exhibit one. Have you testified before?

A. Many times.

Q. What percentage of the cases in which you've testified have been medical malpractice cases as opposed to just giving testimony for a patient of yours in connection with any other kind of case?

A. I would say that most of the cases that I testify in, because of my background as a surgical oncologist, has been as an expert witness in regards to either malpractice or in defense of doctors, so I've testified on both sides in regards to the care of the patient.

Q. Okay. Do you have any idea how often you have testified at a deposition?

A. That would have to be an estimate, but I would say perhaps 25 or 30.

Q. Over what period of time?

A. Thirty-five years. After I became President of the State Division of the American Cancer Society and President of the New England Cancer Society, it's been more frequent.

Q. Okay. You indicated that you testified for both patients as well as physicians in the 25 or 30 cases—

A. That's correct.

Q. What percentage have been for or on behalf of a health care provider?

A. It's almost half and half. I've defended doctors, and I've been called by medical directors of insurance companies to give opinions, and of course a lot of these cases never came to trial.

Q. What is your specialty?

A. I'm a surgical oncologist.

Q. Please define that.

A. When I completed my training in general surgery, I received a National Cancer Institute fellowship to study cancer at Memorial Sloan Kettering Hospital in New York City. I rotated through six different services as the chief resident for six months on each service and did a lot of cancer surgery in each specialty. I spent almost four years in New York City.

Q. Who did you train with?

A. I trained with the top cancer surgeons in the country. Hayes Martin in head and neck surgery, George Pack in gastroenterology surgery, Alexander Brunschwig in Ob-Gyn, John Pool in thorasic surgery, Willet Whitmore in urology and Mike Deddish in colo-rectal surgery.

Q. What qualifies you to be an expert in this case? Prostate cancer -- a urologic problem?

A. I thought you might ask me that question. I brought a letter from Willet Whitmore to show you.

Q. May I see that letter? Mark this letter as <u>exhibit two</u>. It's a letter addressed to Dr. Jack Dixon. Attorney Kirk slowly read the letter... I'll read the bottom paragraph for the record. 'I feel that you have done an outstanding job on my urology service. I've talked to Victor Marshall at New York Hospital and he's willing to take you on his Urology service for one year. after that, I'm inviting you to stay in New York and join my service as a junior attending. Signed Willet Whitmore.'

Q. Why didn't you stay?

A. My wife hated New York City and we had two little children. It wasn't a good place for bringing up kids.

Q. Okay. What happened when you went up to Hartford to practice?

A. I thought I would be accepted with open arms because of my expertise, but I wasn't.

Q. What happened?

A. I applied for surgical privileges at a small hospital on the outskirts of Hartford and was turned down.

Q. Why?

A. The head of the surgical department said I had too much training for their little hospital and I'd be doing all the good, big cases.

Q. What happened when you applied to Hartford Hospital for surgical privileges?

A. That wasn't easy either. I was told I needed an office in town before getting privileges.

Q. With all your training, they wouldn't give you privileges?

A. That's right, so I opened up an office in my home, in an adjorning town. I starved for a year and than I got a break. I ran into Dr. David Burn, the Chief of Urology at Hartford Hospital in the hallway and he talked to me. 'I understand the general surgeons are giving you the business.

You can call it that, I replied.

Well, I don't like that! You can use my office next to the hospital and help me in the O.R. once in a while, said Dr. Burn. You'll have to pay for your phone, however.'

Q. What happened after that?

A. I felt great! I got back into the surgical arena where I could demonstrate my skills. Six months later, I was doing a small case in one of the operating rooms, when one of the senior surgeons in Urology, Dr. Mirabelo, was attempting to do a radical removal of a bladder (cystectomy) in the next O.R.. He got into trouble. He tore a big hole in a large pelvic vein and the patient was bleeding to death. His circulating nurse ran into my room in a panic and asked if I would go help him. When I got there, the belly was filled up with blood and the patient was going into shock. It looked like Dr. Mirabelo was also going into shock along with his resident.

Q. What did you do?

<u>A</u>. I asked for lots of lap pads, they're like towels to soak up blood, and got a bigger suction device to suck out the blood. I told the anesthesiologist to pump the blood into his arm as fast as he could and put a bigger line into one of his veins. Dr. Mirabelo and his resident had been chasing the bleeders without any luck. I cleaned up the mess with the sucker and threw a bunch of pads into the pelvis and applied pressure. I told the circulating nurse to watch the clock for me and tell me when ten minutes was up. I told the anesthesiologist to give more blood to get the patient's blood pressure back to normal. 'Let's stabilize this guy first,' I hollered. ' Everybody take a deep breath and calm down, I said. We're not going to lose this guy!' When the ten minutes were up, I threw the pads out, clamped the big vein that had a hole in it with two vascular DeBakey clamps and quickly sewed the hole up. By this time, Dr. Mirabelo was a basketcase and needed a stiff drink or a cardiac consult. 'Do you want me to complete your operation,' I asked.

'Please,' he replied.

I really enjoyed doing that case and the patient got a beautiful result.   The nessage got around that O.R. and soon I was helping the older urologists and was getting referrals on the big cases... bladders, prostates and kidneys. My practice really got busy.

Q. That was interesting. Any other urology cases?

A. Yes.

Q. Briefly describe it.

A. One of the Obstetricians, Dr. Ed Gibson was diagnosed with a right kidney tumor by one of the younger urologists, Dr. Stalone. Dr. Gibson talked to him and told him that he wanted me to assist on his operation.

'I can handle it myself,' he replied, acting like he was being insulted.

'I want Dixon involved,' he insisted.

'Okay, then you talk to him,' he remarked.

I scrubbed up to help the urologist... it was the first time that I had worked in the O.R. with him. I noticed that as he operated, he was rough in handling the tissues and was in a hurry to get the operation over with. He started to dissect around the outer capsule of the kidney and got into some heavy bleeding. I didn't like it, so I spoke up.

'What are you doing?' I asked.

'I'm dissecting around the kidney.'

"That's not the way I was taught to do it with Whitmore in New York.'

'Okay. Hotshot. What would you do?'

'Most of these patients die with lung metastases,' I replied.

'So what's that got to do with it?'

'Whitmore always dissected out the big right renal vein that enters into the vena cava that goes to the lungs. He ties it off first so that tumor emboli can't get up into the lungs.'

'I don't believe it!'

'Well, believe it or not, I'm leaving the O.R. if you don't do it that way. I don't want to be part of this operation.'

There was a big silence that ensued in that O.R.. You could hear a pin drop. Stalone stopped operating and gave a big sigh. He was unhappy about the rebellious insurgency... finally the silence was broken.

'Okay, you come over on my side of the table and do it. It will be your responsiblity when he dies.'

Q. What happened?

A. I dissected out the renal vein and doubly tied if off with a heavy silk and then removed the kidney.

Q. What happened to the patient?

A. He did well but that's not the end of the story. A month later, Dr. Gibson came into my office with a new full set of golf clubs.

'What's that for?,' I asked.

'The circulating nurse told me you had a fight with Stalone about how to do my operation. I'm glad that you won. Thanks!'

After that, I started getting lots of referrals from that doctor. Gibson lived for fifteen years after that operation.

Q. I guess you do know a little bit about urology. Have you ever testifed in Virginia?

A. No. I have not.

Q. How were you contacted to be an expert in this case?

A. I received a phone call from a prominent lawyer in New York City asking me if I would consider being an expert on a malpractice case in Virginia. Whenever I'm asked this question, I ask for the office and hospital records to look at, and then I decide whether it has any merit or not.

Q. What do you mean by merit?

A. Whether I feel malpractice has occurred or malpractice has not occurred.

Q. Okay, in this case what did you conclude based upon your initial review or your initial discussions by phone?

A. I felt that there was an obvious delay in diagnosis. Would you like me to go into detail about this?

Q. Well, give me a general overview, and then I'm going to come back, and we're going to break it down.

A. Okay. I felt that here's a man who's had kidney stones at an early age and is being followed by a group of urologists, and then he stops seeing them, and then four years ago develops acute

urinary retention with symptoms of rectal fullness and problems

with his prostate gland.

Q. Prostatitis?

A. Prostatitis or whatever.

Q. Well, let me interrupt you there for a second. The what-

ever, do you believe that prostate cancer manifests itself through

specific symptoms?

THE WITNESS: I'll answer that question by saying that

we don't know how prostate cancer develops, and there are a lot of

theories in regards to the etiology. Experts have tried to say that it's

related to genetics, or diet, chronic infection or a lot of different

things. We've been unable to come down with a specific factor that

produces prostate cancer.

BY MR. KIRK:

Q. Okay. Well, what I'm trying to get at is you indicated

that four years ago this patient had come in to see my client. And he had acute urinary retention with some urgency and some fullness that would be consistent with a diagnosis of prostatitis, is that fair?

A. I'd say that it's consistent with that diagnosis, but it could be due to other things such as BPH (hypertrophy of the prostate gland).

Q. Okay. Just because a patient has BPH does not mean that the patient has cancer, though, correct?

A. That's correct. However, it can be! In other words, a patient that comes in with prostate cancer can also have urinary tract retention and can have BPH.

Q. Okay. Do you treat patients from an urological standpoint on a daily basis?

A. I do not at the present time. I told you that I trained under Dr. Whitmore in New York, a famous international Urologist. He devised the Whitmore-Jewett system of staging prostate cancer. It's a system that's used all over the country. When I started practice, I did treat patients with cancer of the bladder, cancer of the kidney, cancer of the prostate, and so forth, because in our area –

the urologists were not trained like I was trained at Sloan Kettering.

So I started teaching the urologists. As a result, I no longer see as

many urology patients, although I have been an expert witness on a

few prostate cancer cases.

Q. Can you tell us about one of those cases?

A. It was a man in his late fifties who had been in an auto-

mobile accident. He had a previously known cancer of the prostate.

A prominent medical oncologist testified that the auto accident dis-

lodged cancer cells from his quiescent cancer of the prostate into

the bones of his pelvis and back. When the patient went into the

E.R., they did numerous x-rays of the bones of his pelvis and back

to check for fractures. When the films were reviewed, there was a

controversy about the findings. Three days later, repeat x-rays were

taken and they clearly showed numerous lytic (washed out) areas in

the bones of his pelvis and back. Blood tests and a biopsy of the

bone defects showed prostate cancer.

Q. What was the controversy about?

<u>A</u>. I was asked if I had seen the x-rays of the patient when he was in the emergency room. I replied and stated that there were lytic washed out areas in the bones at that time.

<u>Q</u>. What happened?

<u>A</u>. Their expert witness, a prominent radiologist, said that he was not sure because there were bowel contents obstructing the views. I disagreed, I replied. Three days later, when they repeated the x-rays, there was definite evidence of bone destruction. "That's exactly what we're talking about," said their attorney. Dr. Roberts, the medical oncologist for the plaintiff, says the auto accident spread the cells to cause those x-ray findings.

<u>Q</u>. What was your response?

<u>A</u>. I told him that it was impossible and ridiculous. I didn't believe it because it takes several months and years to show that much bone destruction from cancer on x-rays. He asked me if I was sure. I said absolutely! If it were trauma that causes the spread of cancer, then anyone in an auto accident would have to be scrutinized closely. We would see a linkage.

Q. What was the outcome?

A. The case was settled out of court and the plaintiff and his lawyer were sued for instituting a frivolous lawsuit.

Q. That's interesting. You would agree with me that there's a big difference in terms of what a surgical oncologist does compared to what an urologist does on a day-to-day basis?"

A. I would agree with that.

Q. Do you ever have patients come to you for treatment with prostatitis?

A. I've seen patients with prostatitis, yes, and I've had patients come in to me who have prostate cancer and have asked me to see them for a second opinion to see if their projected treatment is proper or not. In fact, I have one at the present time. Also, I've seen patients with other types of urological problems.

Q. Give me another example.

A. I had a patient come in about ten years ago at the close of my office hours. He was sixty-five years old. He told me that he had seen three urologists in town that day, and they told him that he needed his bladder removed because of cancer of the bladder. He was a very active man, played golf, fishing etc… and he didn't want to wear a bag after his bladder was removed. I asked him what his tissue diagnosis was. He replied, "cancer of the bladder".

Q. What did you do?

A. I told him to contact the urologists and inform them that I was being consulted for a second opinion. I wanted to see the tissue analysis… the pathology.

Q. What did you find?

A. I showed the microscopic slides to an old, excellent pathologist, Dr. Tennant. He looked at the slides and said that the patient had a very low-grade cancer of the bladder on the surface and the muscle wasn't involved. When I heard that, I told the patient I was sending him to Dr. Whitmore in New York City for a third opinion.

Q. What happened?

A. I received a call from Whitmore in New York City who reviewed the biopsies. He said, 'Jack, you've got to find some honest Urologists up there where you're practicing. The cancers in this man's bladder are very small, like early skin cancers of the face, low-grade basal cell cancers. I'll cauterize (burn) them off. All he needs is a cystoscopy every six months or a little local chemotherapy. He definitely doesn't need his bladder removed... ten years later, he still had his bladder.

Q. You don't see urological patients routinely, do you?

A. No.

BY MR. KIRK:

Q. Well, in this case do you believe that you have enough knowledge to comment on the standard of care for the urologist in terms of treatment based on urological symptoms?

A. Yes. I feel that my training background in urological cancer at Memorial Sloan-Kettering Hospital has qualified me. I have also done quite a bit of cancer research and have served as the President of the New England Cancer Society, which is made up of all of the best cancer specialists in New England. Some are the best in this country.

Q. Well men of all ages come to urologists or to their internist or general practitioner – for problems that relate to their kidneys, bladders or prostate, correct?

A. Right.

Q. Fortunately, there are a vast number of patients out there not because they have prostate cancer, but rather, because they have other urological problems, correct?

A. That's correct.

Q. Prostatitis being one of them, correct?

A. Yes.

Q. Now, you're not advocating that on a patient's first visit to an urologist that an urologist automatically has to suspect that what he is seeing is prostate cancer, are you?

A. No, but I think it should be in his differential diagnosis –

Q. Okay.

A. --if he has acute retention, and this is what this man had.

Q. At what point beginning with that first office visit do you believe that there should have been a diagnosis of prostate cancer by Dr. John Hepburn or a referral to somebody else for that diagnosis if that was what was appropriate?

A. Well, I would like to elaborate just a little bit on this because this man came in and was treated for prostatitis, and he was treated with Septra, an antibiotic, and he had repeated visits to the urologist for prostate massage. Then he was treated with Tetracycline, another antibiotic and he did not do well, and later he was treated with Cipro, which means that he was treated with three different antibiotics over a period of about a year and a half. Obviously, the urologist should have been aware of the fact that the prostatitis was not responding to the antibiotic therapy, and should have been thinking about doing a cystoscopy probably at an earlier date than was done. He also should have thought about the possibility of things like BPH, enlargement of his prostate, and cancer, and he should have done a blood test, a prostatic stimulating antigen test, which has been around since 1986. I think that test would have been abnormal at that time, and it would have given him a hint to do further testing to see why he wasn't doing well.

Q. All right. You agreed with me that merely because a patient presents with symptoms consistent with prostatitis there's no reason to believe on that occasion that the patient has prostate cancer?

A. That's at the first visit. That's correct.

Q. All right. At what point in time do you believe that any further diagnostic treatment was necessary in order to make a differential diagnosis concerning prostate cancer, what date?

A. You're asking me to give one specific date?

Q. Well, you can give me a date; you can give me a month.

A. I would say he should have had a cystoscopy sooner than a year and a half. I would say that it probably should have been done in six months. Mr. Johnston saw Dr. John Hepburn, seven times in the first six months. That's a lot of visits!

Q. Now, are you talking about a cystoscopy?

A. Yes, because a cystoscopy is going to give him an opportunity to look at the median lobe of the prostate. It might have given him some feeling about whether further testing should

be done and whether a biopsy might be appropriate.

Q. All right, so you think that a cystoscopy should have

been done at about six months, it would have been –

A. Would have been nice. It's a simple procedure. It actu-

ally can be done in an office or as an outpatient. It would have

probably given him some insight into whether he was dealing with

prostatitis or whether he was dealing with BPH, because when he

did the cystoscopy, I notice that in the records he stopped giving

antibiotics and he changed his diagnosis from prostatitis to BPH, so

now you're dealing with two different things. He obviously is now

starting to think, "Well now, here's a guy who has acute retention,

and suddenly he doesn't have prostatitis, he's got something else

going on, he's got BPH. Maybe we should look into why he has

BPH." 48 or 50 is young for getting BPH, and you have to have a

high titer of suspicion, I think, as a good urologist to think about

cancer.

Q. 48 to 50 is very young for prostate cancer, isn't that right?

A. That's exactly right.

Q. Well, would you agree with me that a biopsy would have only been warranted if there was something suspicious that showed up in the cystoscopy?

A. No. I would say that the prostatic stimulating antigen should have been done also, so that if that was negative, I'd say I agree with you, but if that was elevated, I'd say no.

Q. Okay. Do you believe that the biopsy or the PSA test should have been done contemporaneously –or contemporaneous with the cystoscopy or later?

THE WITNESS: I would have done the PSA before the cystoscopy because instrumentation causes an elevation of the PSA.

Q. What was his grade on the Gleason Scale?

A. Why are you asking me this question?

Q. Isn't the severity of prostate cancer determined by the Gleason Scale?

A. It doesn't apply in this case. No biopsies were done for four years, and when it was done, he had a Stage IV advanced cancer. You have to do a biopsy and Pathologists have to grade the tissue reviewed under a microscope (two specimens)... Grades 2 through 4 are low and 7 to 10 are high. The fact that he didn't have a Gleason's Scale early on, tells you that they didn't do a biopsy and that they goofed.

Q. I understand... scratch that question. Are you aware of what was being done in the medical community in Richmond in terms of PSA testing?

A. I would say no because I don't practice there. However, I would say that on a national basis, most of the counties in this country would be doing PSAs when indicated.

Q. Is your opinion consistent with the recommendations of the American Urological Society or the Association?

A. It may not be the opinion of the American Urological Society because I don't know their recommendations, but it is the opinion of the American Cancer Society.

Q. Are you familiar with what the recommendations are of the American Urological Association, concerning the use of the PSA test as a screening device for a particular patient for the presence of prostate cancer?

A. You're talking about screening. Screening is different than somebody that comes in with symptoms. If a person comes in with symptoms of retention or BPH or what was diagnosed as a persistent prostatitis, for a year and a half, that individual, I feel, should have a PSA test. It's not a screening test. A screening test is where you take a large group of people and do the test to see what your yield is going to be in regards to prostate cancer. That yield is going to be very low. But if you take a group of people with symptoms, your yield is going to be much higher. You have to define what the specific patient's symptoms are before you can determine whether they should have a PSA test or not.

Q. Well, in this particular patient when was it, based upon your reading of the records, that there was a diagnosis of BPH?

A. When he did the cystoscopy – a year and a half after the onset of his symptoms.

Q. Do you know Dr. George Ewing, who is the Chief of Urologic Surgery at the University Hospital in Washington, D.C.?

A. Yes, I am aware of Dr. Ewing, and he's an outstanding Urologist. I don't know him personally, but I do know that he has done research in the area of prostate cancer and particularly in regards to surgery of prostate cancer.

Q. Have you read his deposition in this case?

A. I have not read his deposition.

Q. Has anybody explained to you how he has testified at his deposition?

A. Not really. I do not have a copy of it, and I haven't reviewed it.

Q. Okay. Dr. Dixon, are you aware of the fact that he is now treating the plaintiff, Mr. Johnston for his prostate cancer?

<u>A</u>. Yes, I am. I am aware of the fact that he's getting Ulexin, and I'm aware of the fact that his PSA has dropped down to 6.5.

<u>Q</u>. If Dr. Ewing has testified in his deposition which I took over at the University Hospital a couple of weeks ago, that in his opinion that even if there had been an earlier diagnosis of Mr. Johnston's prostate cancer that it would have made no difference whatsoever in terms of Mr. Johnston's ultimate outcome and his survivability, would you agree with him?

<u>A</u>. No! I would say that I don't know how he can make that statement. I would not agree with him!

<u>Q</u>. Why?

<u>A</u>. The reason is that what he's doing is he's projecting life expectancy based on seeing a patient at the University Hospital, after the fact. He did not see the patient earlier, when he first got sick. He did not see the stage of disease which the urologist, Dr. Hepburn had seen. Dr. Hepburn didn't even stage his disease because he missed it cold. When he finally made the diagnosis, the

cancer was out of bounds, a Stage four cancer. His glands and bones were diffusely involved.

Q. Well, we know what the PSA test levels were when they were first obtained. You agree with that?

A. I agree with that. However, that was four years after he was first seen.

Q. And the average PSA test at that point was between fifteen and sixteen hundred, is that your recollection?

A. That's right.

Q. Were you aware of the fact that he had been on Proscar for a number of months before the PSA level was tested?

A. Yes, I am aware of that fact.

Q. And are you also aware of the effect that Proscar has on a patient's PSA levels?

A. It can cause a slight elevation, that's correct. But not an elevation of fifteen hundred or sixteen hundred. When you get an elevation of a PSA at that level, you can predict that the patient already has gland and bone metastases.

Q. You don't agree that it does; you just agree that it can?

A. Yes, that's correct. It's more apt to lower it.

Q. All right. Now, were you aware that in part, Dr. Ewing's analysis was based upon looking at the PSA level as measured after his cystoscopy in Los Angeles, assuming, based upon statistical information, what the doubling time was of the PSA level, and then extrapolating that to what the PSA level was as early as when he was first seen. Were you aware that that was in part the analysis that he's made?

A. I'm not aware of that, but I'm not so sure that you can statistically make that analysis and use it as a predictable measure of the stage of the disease. I think that going backwards from a PSA level, which is a laboratory finding, and saying that that level four years ago would have been elevated if he had done a PSA, to me what that does, that incriminates the urologist for not having done a PSA when he was first seen, which he could have done. It shows that the Urologist was not conforming to what a normal urologist should be doing in that time frame in the diagnosis of the urological problem that this man had.

Q. Dr. Dixon, are you aware of the fact that Dr. Ewing believes that in his opinion, based upon the type of analysis that I just gave to you, is in fact supported by all of the clinical and the research data that they have accumulated at the University Medical Center?

A. Could you show me that?

Q. Do I have the clinical and research data here today?

A. Right, yes.

Q. No, I don't. If Dr. Ewing has testified that that is consistent with all of his clinical experience as well as the vast body of literature that has been written, as well as research data accumulated at the University Hospital would you disagree with him on that?

A. You'd have to verify your statement. I would want to see the research before I would answer that question.

Q. Why?

<u>A</u>. My interpretation of Dr. Ewing's research might be different than yours. Besides, if you did a PSA test when he was first seen with prostatitis... prostatitis can cause an elevated PSA... that would be a fudge factor in Dr. Ewing's opinion.

<u>Q</u>. Okay. Well, do you read "The New England Journal of Medicine"?

<u>A</u>. All the time. I've been the lead author of two research papers in that journal.

<u>Q</u>. Are you familiar with any publications in that journal pertaining to prostate cancer?

<u>A</u>. Yes.

<u>Q</u>. Okay. There is an article that appeared in the New England Journal of Medicine entitled "Results of Conservative Management of Clinically Localized Prostate Cancer," Dr. Chodak, C-H-O-D-A-K, and others. Are you familiar with that article?

<u>A</u>. I think I've read it. I've looked at it. I usually read the summaries and conclusions. Let's see. Let me think for a minute.

Let me try to recall. It's about hormone treatment for early stage one prostate cancer which I think this man had when first seen.

Q. You think he had what?

A. I think he had Stage I or Stage II prostate cancer. I believe that his prostate cancer was localized to the gland. It had not spread.

Q. How can you say that? What specifically do you believe supports that conclusion?

A. Well, the Urologist makes a diagnosis of prostatitis and treats the patient with three different antibiotics and massages the gland on numerous occasions for a year and a half. He describes the prostate as a normal boggy gland. Because he's not getting better, he takes a look in the bladder (cystoscopy) and states that the gland has doubled in size. He changes his diagnosis to benign prostatic hypertrophy (BPH). He sees the patient for another two years and on numerous occasions does not describe any change in the prostate gland. If there's a cancer there, it's still within the gland – a Stage I or Stage II cancer. Now four years later, while speaking in

L.A., he has acute urinary retention, collapses and is taken to the E.R. at UCLA Hospital where a diagnosis of prostate cancer is made. He returns to his Urologist in Richmond for a work-up and Dr. Hepburn signs a sheet saying that the patient has an advanced cancer of the prostate, Stage IV, one of the worst cancers, and that the cancer extends through the prostatic capsule and has spread into the lymph glands (inguinal groin area) and outside the pelvis areas, and in his report he questions the bone metastases, which I don't question at all.

Q. You disagree with Dr. Hepburn?

A. Yes.

I've shown these x-rays to our radiologist, and there's no doubt that this man had spread of his cancer (bone and glandular metastases) when he had a biopsy four years after his prostatitis. He's now a D stage cancer of the prostate, which means that his life expectancy is less than three years.

Q. What should they have done earlier?

A. After six months had passed, they should have done diagnostic testing. When you look at the bone x-rays on this man, in order to show a lesion in bone, that lesion has to be over 1.2 or 1.3 millimeters in size. The cancer has to wash out 50 percent of that area in order for it to show up on an x-ray. It takes approximately two years for a bone lesion to reach that size. And these lesions measure approximately that size, which means that this patient, if you go back and just look at those x-rays, you can tell that two years ago he was getting a progression of his disease from an early stage to an advanced stage.

Q. What would his life expectancy be at that time?

A. It would be 10 to 12 years.

Q. How do you know that?

A. Statistics will show you that in the literature.

Q. Are you able to determine what the staging level was of this man's cancer when he had his cystoscopy, Dr. Dixon?

A. You have to go by what the urologist states in his examination of the prostate, he keeps saying it's a boggy prostate. He doesn't feel anything outside the capsule, it's an early stage lesion. If it's a C lesion, in which he does describe it later on, then it's grown outside the capsule of the prostate. It involves the seminal vesicles around the prostate. And, so all the time he was massaging this gland, he keeps saying the disease was confined to the prostate gland –whatever it was, was in the prostate. It wasn't outside the capsule. So what you're dealing with is an early lesion (A-B).

Q. I just want to make sure I understand –that your sole basis for saying what his life expectancy was as at the time of the cystoscopy was the clinical notes of Dr, Hepburn concerning his examination of the prostate gland and his description of it, is that correct?

A. That's one of the things.

Q. Okay.

A. I also think that since he did not have a PSA, you cannot use conjecture and go back from a PSA of 1200 or 1600 and say that the PSA at that time is going to be a certain amount.

Q. Why not?

A. Because I've seen patients that have prostate cancer that have a 10, and they have metastatic disease, and it doesn't show 1200 or 1400. The PSA measures the prostate tissue itself, and it also tells you whether the prostate shows residual disease. However, it does not always tell you when there's bony metastases. In other words, you can have a PSA of 14 and still have bony metastases.

Q. Okay. The New England Journal article that I've just put in front of you, on the first page I have highlighted the last part of the sentence in the first paragraph which states: "We do not know whether early detection will reduce mortality." Do you agree with that statement?

A. I would agree with that. I think that prostate cancer is controversial, and the treatment methods are controversial, and the diagnosis methods are undergoing great change at the present time. But I do think that each case is specific, and you apply the knowledge that we have today with each case, and in this case it's obvious. Here's a man who comes in with acute retention, who probably did not have an advanced lesion when he came in. And then the disease progressed on while this guy was massaging him. The massage was not helping this patient. All you have to think about is cells getting free into the circulation and lymphatics, every time you massage that guy for a year or a year and a half. He was feeding cancer cells into those lymphatic glands or blood stream. When you massage a prostate, you push hard with your digital finger all around that gland, to try to empty it out. It can be painful! What you've got here is a progression of a lesion that probably was in the median lobe because he couldn't feel it when he did a rectal exam and that's why he should have done a cystoscopy earlier. He should have done an ultrasound and a biopsy at that time, and he probably would have picked it up, and given him a longer life expectancy. We do know one thing, and that is that prostate cancer is a more serious disease in a young person than it is in the older person, and this is why we tell people when they get over 70 if they get an early lesion (A-! or A-11) lesion that maybe they don't need any treatment at all. But we're more aggressive in the treatment of young patients that have prostate cancer. They may need radical surgery, a radical prostatectomy, sometimes followed by radiation therapy. The radiation therapy can be seed implants or external radiation or both.

Q. And in fairness, wouldn't it also make sense or wouldn't the flip side of that coin, Dr. Dixon, be that it's impossible for you to sit here and say that earlier detection of this patient's prostate cancer would have changed his outcome from the disease?

A. No! I would say that in all probability it would have changed the outcome because of the fact that the urologist kept feeling that gland, and that gland did not show anything outside the capsule. We know that when you get prostate cancer outside the capsule, the prognosis is going to be much worse. This urologist kept feeling this gland and saying this is prostatitis, and he kept writing in his notes that it was a boggy gland, and says it gets twice its size. So there was a growth factor. The growth factor in a man 50 years old is a little bit unusual.

Q. Is it your belief that the only way that prostate cancer spreads is by an extrusion through the capsule around the prostate, that it cannot metastasize in any other means?

A. No. Prostate cancer spreads by three different ways, local extension is the <u>first</u>. It can grow into the seminal vesicle around the gland. This is usually determined by digital examination or ultrasound. It's bad when this happens but not the worse. It's called C Stage. <u>Second</u>. It can spread through lymphatic channels to lymph glands inside the pelvis or abdomin. This is diagnosed by CAT scans, MRIs or by looking inside the abdomin with a laporascope. <u>Third</u>. It can get into the bloodsteam and get into the bones or other organs. This can be determined by bone scans or x-rays. This is D stage.

Q. Now, which of those methods are you, as the examining physician, going to be able to detect when you do a digital examination of the prostate gland?

A. Usually local extension, and if you're not sure, if you have a persistent symptom, then you do a cystoscopy to look at the median lobe, and if you're still not sure, then you biopsy the entire gland by transrectal ultrasound to see what you've got. And when the doctor at UCLA did that, all areas of that prostate were involved with cancer. All six needle biopsies were positive. In fact, I'm surprised they never did a CAT scan or an MRI in this case.

Q. Was there lymphatic or hematologic progression of his disease?

THE WITNESS: Well, obviously it was because the glands were positive when he had his laparoscopy. In fact, you can question whether they should have even done a laparoscopy at all... in view of the fact that his bone scans were positive. In fact, if you read the op note dictated by Dr. Hepburn, the op note says that they were going to do a laparoscopy to biopsy the glands, and if the glands were negative, they were going to do a prostatectomy from inside.

BY MR KIRK:

Q. Now, this is when they biopsied the gland.

A. That's exactly right. But you're asking me about the thinking of these people. They were out of it. I'm saying that with a positive x-ray and bone scan, they shouldn't have even been thinking about doing a prostatectomy. They should have been thinking about treating him with hormones and doing an orchiectomy right off the bat. The horse was already out of the barn.

Q. Well, let me ask you, you don't believe that there were any deviations from the standard of care concerning the treatment for the diagnosed cancer when the biopsy was done that had any impact on this man's outcome?

A. No, I don't. but, it was at least three and a half years too late.

Q. I understand the point that you just made. Now is it not true that because we know that there was lymphatic and hematologic involvement that the spread of the cancer through the lymph nodes and the spread of the cancer into the bloodstream can in and of itself mean that this man has a fatal outcome to look forward to for his prostate cancer?

A. Yes.

Q. If Dr. Hepburn had, as you say, picked up through his digital examination that this disease process was breaking out through the prostate gland, how can you tell at that point whether there was lymphatic or hematologic involvement?

A. Do a CT Scan or MRI. If the x-rays and MRI are negative, we know that in C stage with proper treatment of the prostate gland and there's no evidence of bone metastases, you can get a much better prognosis than if the lymph nodes or the bone marrow is involved by cancer. So that even at a C stage when it gets outside of the capsule, you can still salvage and get better results with proper treatment, either a radical prostatectomy or radiation therapy or both. Do you understand what I'm saying?

Q. You're not suggesting that the patient could have been cured of the cancer at that point, are you?

A. No.

Q. Okay.

A. But he could have gotten a longer survival time, five or ten years.

THE WITNESS: I would say that, that this man progressed from an A to a B to a C, and then a D stage. He had a cystoscopy, he didn't have any PSAs, and then the urologist says he has a C stage when he makes his diagnosis four years later. If he did not have nodes in the lymphatics that were positive and if he did not have bone metastases, at that time, even in a C stage he has a pretty good chance of getting a pretty good survival.

BY MR.KIRK:

Q. Assume for the sake of my question that in the beginning there was lymphatic involvement and/or hematologic involvement. Now, if that were true, would this man's outcome be any different if the cancer had been detected in the beginning as opposed to it having been detected four years later?

A. That's a hypothetical question because we don't have all the facts. We don't have a prostatic stimulating antigen blood test that was measured in the beginning. We do not have any biopsies that were done, so I can't answer that question.

Q. Well, I'm just asking –

A. You're asking for a hypothetical answer, which I can't give.

Q. Why not?

A. The staging is very important. I don't think anybody staged this patient back at the beginning, because they didn't think he had cancer. You have to go by the digital rectal examination of the urologist who was doing prostatic massage, and he kept describing a boggy gland that was twice its size, and he doesn't say anything of it being outside of the capsule. Therefore, you can't stage it as a C stage, and you can't stage it as a D stage.

Q. But you had previously agreed with me that the digital examinations of the prostate gland in no way is a determiner or an indicator of whether there is lymphatic or hematologic involvement of the disease?

A. That's correct. You have to do a CAT scan, MRI or laparaoscopy and biopsy.

Q. Okay.

A. I want to say one other thing. Can I answer –

Q. Sure.

A. The two best ways that we now feel that you can detect prostate cancer is by digital rectal examination combined with a PSA. What happened here is that the Urologist did not do a PSA or a digital rectal examination that was accurate. Therefore, what he was doing, he was not conforming with what is the best way of detecting prostate cancer. He didn't do his job.

Q. You believe that all urologists would agree with you on that?

A. Yes.

MEDICAL SUPREME COURT
CHIEF JUSTICE JACKSON:

"The defense may now state their arguments."

<u>Mr. David Kirk:</u> "Your Honor, we feel that the Medical Supreme Court should not be adjudicating this case. In fact, we thought that the court would refuse to hear it. In Richmond, this case was not decided because it was a 'hung jury'. The jury foreman said that they didn't understand the important issues that could decide whether there was malpractice or not."

"Did the judge instruct the jury properly?" asked Jackson.

"We thought he did. They still couldn't reach a unanimous decision."

"We thought that it would be remanded to the State Supreme Court."

<u>Chief Justice Jackson:</u> "Mr. Kirk, in the 37th Amendment to the Constitution, it clearly states that the Medical Supreme Court will have the final juridiction over major malpractice cases that have been heard at the state District or Appellate Court Level and then appealed. Which is exactly what has happened... State your defense."

<u>Mr. Kirk:</u> "Your Honor, we feel that Dr. Hepburn was presented with a difficult case to handle. The Senator is a prominent individual who presented with acute urinary retention and had a large boggy gland that was extremely tender due to prostatitis. It was hard to determine just what was going on. The prostatitis masked the tumor growing in his gland. "

<u>Associate Justice John Whipple:</u> "Mr. Kirk, I'm a general practitioner who has seen prostatitis in my practice. I usually do a rectal exam, start the patient on antibiotics and if he doesn't respond in 6-8 weeks, refer the patient to a urologist. Usually the

urologist that I deal with, if the prostatitis persists, does a cystoscopy or an ultrasound and biopsy. I'm surprised that the expert, Dr. Hepburn, treated this patient for prostatitis for a year and a half without doing a more extensive work-up including a P.S.A test."

Mr. Kirk: "As you know, the prostate is very tender when you have prostatitis. All you have to do is touch it and the patient tries to wiggle away. It's difficult to stage the patient in this situation."

Associate Justice Whipple: "Yes, but you've forgotten that Dr. Hepburn was massaging this gland to try to empty the pus out. He got a good feel of that gland on numerous occasions."

Associate Justice Sanchez: "I'm surprised that Dr. Hepburn didn't do a P.S.A. test even after doing the cystoscopy a year and one-half later."

Mr. Kirk: "Your Honor, my client, Dr. John Hepburn, belongs to several H.M.O.'s and they do not pay for the blood P.S.A. test for screening for prostate cancer. That's probably why he didn't do it."

Associate JusticeSanchez: "But this test was a diagnostic test, wasn't it? It wasn't a screening test."

Mr. Kirk: "You can debate that issue, your Honor, since the patient when he was first seen, was only 48-years-old. He's young for prostate cancer."

Associate Justice Sanchez: "He's also a U.S. Senator, Mr. Kirk. In retrospect, I'm sure he'd be willing to pay for a P.S.A. test if need be. If it had been done earlier, treatment could have had a profound effect on his life expectancy."

Mr. Kirk: "Your Honor, we feel that Senator Johnston was an extremely difficult patient to examine adequately because he was obese and difficult to deal with."

Chief Justice Jackson: "That should have been all the more reason to do more diagnostic testing... none was done. Only one cystoscopy in three and one half years."

Mr. Kirk: "Your Honor, we also feel that Senator Johnston could have had an advanced prostate cancer when he was first seen by Dr. Hepburn."

Chief Justice Jackson: "There are no facts to substantiate that. Nothing written in the chart, to suggest that... Dr. Hepburn felt that prostate gland thirty or forty times. Three and one-half years later, a young resident at UCLA's Hospital E.R. examined him and established a diagnosis of prostate cancer. An M.R.I. and CT scan showed advanced D. stage prostate cancer. When you look at Dr. Hepburn's written chart, he saw Senator Johnston only three months earlier."

Mr. Kirk: "Your Honor, it was difficult to perform necessary tests because Senator Johnston was not readily available for testing."

Chief Justice Jackson: "Mr. Kirk, how can you say that? I have gone over all the material necessary to reach a judgement in this case, with my law clerk, including Dr. Jack Dixon's testimony, and it appears to me that there was a delay in diagnosis and that your client Dr. John Hepburn did not conform to the standards expected of Urologists that practice in this day and age. I'm surprised that a settlement did not occur at the level of the District Court."

Mr. Kirk: "I hate to bring this up, your Honor, but the Insurance Companies are refusing to pay the big settlement. The plaintiffs want fair, just, and reasonable damages for past and future economic and non-economic damages. His wife wants additional damages for loss of consortium."

Chief Justice Jackson: "What are they asking for?"

Mr. Kirk: "Five million dolllars."

Chief Justice Jackson: "Mr. Packard, will your client settle for less?"

Mr. Packard: "The Senator's wife is very upset and wants full payment. She also wanted the case presented to the Medical Supreme Court, so that the media and public could learn more about prostate cancer."

Chief Justice Jackson: "Her attitude is commendable but it should not interfere with the judgment of this court. She got the wish of having our Medical Supreme Court adjudicate this case. If she gets five million, your law firm will be well compensated. Isn't that correct?"

Mr. Packard: "Yes, Your Honor."

Chief Justice Jackson: "Do any of the other Associate Justices have anymore questions? "
There were none.

The Medical Supreme Court voted in favor of the plaintiff, Senator Sam Johnston... eight to one. However, the court felt that the punitive damages were excessive. They reduced the award to one million dollars.

12

SURPRISE AND REELECTION PLANS

Kelli was near the end of her third year of her Presidency and the Party's Chairmen was beginning to think about the Presidential election that would be coming up the following fall. She would be running for reelection and was considered a strong candidate with high poll ratings... a shoo-in. The Republicans were probably going to put up Preston Adams again, the Senate Majority Leader.

Kevin Powers, the Democratic Party Chairmen, called Kelli and requested a private meeting to discuss reelection plans. They met for lunch at the Hotel Mayflower in downtown Washington, D.C.

"I'm going on a vacation to Hawaii in three weeks. Your campaigning will have to be put on the back burner."

"No problem," he replied. "After you get back, you'll be well rested to start our Party's campaign drive for your reelection."

"Kevin, there's something that I want to talk to you about. I've done almost all the things I've wanted to do. Do I really have to run for reelection?"

"Yes! You owe it to the Party," he replied.

"My husband and children don't want me to run. The subject of reelection has been a point of contention recently at our family gatherings. I don't have any personal family life any more."

"They're wrong! You're young, you're intelligent, you're vibrant, you've done a great job and you've accomplished a lot, and you're a woman. You owe it to the Party and for all women to run for reelection."

"I won't argue the point. We can talk about it some more when I get back from my vacation."

"What are the political pundits predicting?" she asked

"Well, they're going to be out to get you because of that Constitutional Convention that you successfully engineered. Ninety Congressman, seventy Representatives and twenty Senators were over the term limits and had to leave."

"I expected that! I consider that my greatest challenge and greatest achievement."

"That isn't all. Twenty more were thrown out because of poor health. They didn't want to go before the Medical Supreme Court."

"You made lots of enemies by what you did and almost got killed."

"That's a hazard that every President faces."

"All those retired Senators and Representatives are an unhappy lot."

"They got what they deserved. They were on ego trips. If they weren't millionaires when they went in, they were when they got out. They created the stagnation in Congress. We've got some real energetic Congressmen now."

"The trial lawyers are really upset about that Medical Supreme Court."

"I don't worry about that either. We have too many lawyers in Congress. They're not a fair representation of the people. Our founding fathers would not approve of that."

"The Medical Supreme Court is doing what it is suppose to do. It's functioning properly. I don't feel sorry for them."

"Campaign Finance Reform with a limit on expenditures is going to make it tough to get the message out to the public. We're going to have to be very selective in how we use that money for advertising."

"That's what's suppose to happen. We have a level playing field now."

"There still are some other things for you to do."

"I know. One is selection of the candidates for the Presidency. The primary system as it now exists stinks. Determining the candidates at a convention is more realistic, exciting and honest."

"Why don't you have a press conference before you go?"

"That's not a bad idea. Senator Sam Johnston's trial at the Medical Supreme Court has engendered quite a bit of discussion on the nightly primetime TV and in the newspapers. I'd like to clarify my opinion. The New York Times and the *Washington Post* documented the entire proceedings."

PRESS CONFERENCE
WHITE HOUSE PRESS ROOM

Kelli made a few opening remarks.

"Members of the press, I decided to have this press conference so that you could be fully informed about my feelings concerning recent events that have taken place. I'll take your questions."

Marilyn Osborn, the head of the press corps was recognized. "Ms. President, I wonder if you would comment about the Senator Johnston case. The tort lawyers are concerned about the Medical Supreme Court's decision, particularly the reduction in punitive damages."

Kelli: *"I was hoping that you would ask that question. The Johnston case demonstrates the complexity of medical malpractice lawsuits and why the Medical Supreme Court was needed. The lawyers in the lower courts and the judges did not have the scientific knowledge to adjudicate this case properly. If you read the New York Times or Washington's Post documentation of the proceedings, you can readily see how complicated a medical malpractice can be. This case is about prostate cancer that kills many of the men in our society. I thought that Dr. Dixon's expertise was quite evident in his deposition. Some of the questions asked by the defense lawyers were inappropriate and did not relate to the evaluation of malpractice. It's obvious that the judge at the district court level and the defense lawyers didn't understand the causality, the interrelationship of Dr. Hepburn's poor repeated physical examinations and massage of the patient for a prolonged period of time (3 1/2 years) and the effect it had on the patient's life expectancy. If that patient had proper evaluation and testing early on, a P.S.A. test and proper staging of his disease, he would still be in the Senate today."*

"As for the punitive damages being reduced. There should be a practical limit to the amount awarded. Exorbitant awards just raise the cost of health care that you and I have to pay for."

Marilyn Osborn: "I'd like a follow-up, Ms. President. You did not address why the court reduced the punitive damages in this case."

"I'll address that issue... it was too high! In some cases, the punitive damage awards are outrageously ridiculous. A woman in a fast-food restaurant spilled hot coffee on herself and got burned and was awarded one million dollars by a jury. That case should have been thrown out by the judge and she and her lawyers should have had to pay the court costs. Some states actually have limits in the amount that can be awarded. I agree with the states but not

totally. The awards have to be realistic. There are too many medical malpractice lawsuits!"

Bob Watson of the *St. Louis Post* was recognized.

"Ms. President, Senator Bond as you know, was one of the oldest members of the Senate, serving for more than 40+ years... now he's out of the Senate. In his recent interview on TV, he castigated you for limiting the Senator's term to eighteen years. He said you were destroying this country's political stability. He emphasized that his experience was invaluable to the Senate."

"I disagree, and you can debate his statement. If you can't learn how to work in the Senate in eighteen years, you don't belong there. New fertile, innovative minds are necessary to maintain strength and diversity in this country and to be utilized in the Senate.

Senator Bond has been an excellent Senator. I believe he is almost ninety years old. If he wasn't removed because of term limits, he probably would be removed for failure to pass a routine physical exam. I believe he's had a pacemaker put in because of fainting spells caused by a slow pulse. Repeated episodes can cause brain damage."

Don Caldwell from the *Denver Post* was next.

"Ms. President, you will be up for reelection next year. Are you planning to run?"

"Yes. I am definitely planning to run, although I feel I have accomplished quite a bit. Getting the states to have a Constitutional Convention has been the highlight of my career."

"I'd like a follow-up," he replied.

"Haven't you been going too fast? Aren't all these changes disruptive?"

"No," she replied. "When that Constitution was written, there were thirteen states and only about two to three million people in this country. The founding fathers were mainly property owners and they were religious people. They knew that this country would grow, and diversity in the populace would develop. There are fifty states now and two hundred and seventy million people.

They wrote into that Constitution, two different ways to amend it and that's what we did!"

June Briggs of the *Boston Globe* spoke up.

"Ms. President, I understand that you'll be going on a vacation soon. What are your plans?"

"Probably Hawaii. I need a little rest to recharge my batteries."

Kelli, Mark and the two children flew on U.S. Air Force One to Barber's Point Naval Air Station in Hawaii and then took a helicopter to Maui. They would be vacationing on a palatial estate with private beaches near Kapalua Beach and, next to a beautiful golf course. The Secret Service accompanied them and Vice President Brian Hatfield was more than happy to run the government back in Washington, D.C. Most of the world's major powers were digesting the results of their recent summit meeting. China had withdrawn its forces off the coast of Taiwan and the Philippines, and on the world front, there were a few small skirmishes, but no major problems.

The family really needed a vacation together. In the morning they went to the beautiful sandy beaches and in the afternoon they either played golf, tennis or went fishing. Kelli was briefed by her press secretary in the late afternoon about current important world affairs and communications from world leaders.

One morning, the two children went by helicopter with the Secret Service to the Barber's Point Naval Air Station. From there, they went to see the Navy National World War II Memorial -- the U.S.S. Arizona that was sunk when Pearl Harbor was attacked. The children stayed overnight at the Barber's Point Naval Base so they could go shopping and to the beaches at Diamond Head the next day.

It was a perfect time for Mark and Kelli to be alone and renew their love relationship. Kelli's personnel secretary had bought her some new bathing suits and leisurewear for the occasion. After breakfast, Kelli put on a black bikini with a cover-up. Mark got into his trunks and they went to the beach. He carried a cocktail jug of daiquiris with him.

"The first time we got together, we drank daiquiris. Do you remember?" asked Mark.

"Of course!" she said with a smile. "You got me drunk and took advantage of me."

"No way," replied Mark.

"How could I forget? I also wore a black bikini like the one I'm wearing now."

"You're still as beautiful. Now that I've got my wife back, I plan to make sure that she gets enough exercise on vacation and that includes sex."

"I'm all for it," replied Kelli. "The more the merrier."

They found a secluded spot on the beach and after swimming in the water; they talked and had a couple of drinks. It wasn't long before their bathing suits came off.

"The Secret Service will be watching us," said Kelli. "I'll bet there's a submarine with a periscope or some Navy Seals out there too!"

"Let 'em watch," he replied. "They might learn something. I talked to our Chief Secret Service Agent who is with us and told him that we wanted to have complete privacy on the beach while the children were gone."

"No problem, I understand," he replied.

"You stinker! You planned this."

"That's right," said Mark. "Are you complaining?"

"I must admit, I'm finally completely relaxed."

"We have all afternoon and evening together alone."

"You're really in a macho mood, aren't you?"

During the afternoon and evening, Mark pursued her and finally at 4:00 A.M. when Mark approached her again, she asked for restraint. I'm exhausted," she said. "You prepared for this. I heard that you jogged everyday for a month before we started our vacation. That gives you an unfair advantage. The next time, I'll jog with you so that I can keep up with you."

The leaders of the Democratic Party in Congress threw a party for her at the Willard Inter-Continental Hotel in Washington when Kelli and Mark got back. It wasn't just for fun, because you had to ante up $1,000 to attend. The money would be put in the Party's coffers to help finance the upcoming Presidential election. Kelli's speech to the Party's faithful was fantastic... she was completely relaxed following her vacation and was able to get the large crowd into a jovial mood. Journalists attending the meeting were impressed and felt that she would be hard to beat.

"Who do you think the Republicans will have for their standard bearer?" she asked Powers.

"It will be a wide open race, but because Preston Adams gave you a good race, he'll probably get the nod."

"How old is Preston now?"

"I think he's seventy-one."

"Well, he couldn't be a Supreme Court Justice," remarked Kelli, with a smile on her face. "You know, Kevin, the best thing I've done as President, was to get all those states to agree to get together and have a Constitutional Convention. Congress was afraid we'd rewrite the Constitution, but we didn't."

"We now have healthier people running this government," remarked Kevin. "I think that's important, too. How do you feel, Kelli?"

"I feel great, although, I've gained a little weight. One of these days I'll go through the menopause."

"When's your next physical exam?"

"In January," she replied.

When Kelli saw her medical doctor at Bethesda Naval Hospital in January, she had a complete physical examination.

"Ms. President, I find you in excellent health. There's just one thing. I've noticed some changes in your breasts and in your pelvic exam. I believe you're about three-and-a-half months pregnant. We'll do some blood tests and an ultrasound to confirm it, but I think I can hear a little heartbeat."

Kelli's face turned white and then she blushed, bright red.

"Oh, my goodness! It can't be! That would mean I'd have the baby while I'm still in the White House."

"That's right," said Dr. Lucille Berger.

"I suppose there will be a media uproar when my physical examination results are released."

"I think something like that will happen."

"Well, believe it or not, I'm happy about what you've just told me. Now I'm sure I won't run for reelection and I have a good excuse. I thought I might be going through an early menopause when I missed those periods and gained some weight."

Kelli met with Kevin and gave him the news about her pregnancy.

"I'm not going to run for reelection!"

"You really don't mean that, do you? Let's give it some serious thought, first. If you don't run, the Party's got a big problem."

"Not really," replied Kelli. "We have many qualified candidates."

"We can't release the news to the public until we've all had a chance to think about this," emphasized Kevin.

"I'm very happy about it. I have to release the news."

"Do you really want another baby at your age?"

"Are you inferring that I should have an abortion?"

"No. Not at all. But that could be an option."

"Not in my book!" replied Kelli... her eyes flashing. "I'm not showing my pregnancy yet, although, I have gained weight and will begin to show in the midriff soon. I'd like to announce it in a press conference as soon as possible."

"Before you do that, Kelli, I think that we should have a meeting of the party's notables to discuss this calamity in an open forum to determine what's the best way to approach this."

"Are you kidding?" replied Kelli. "It's not a calamity. It's an exciting joyous occasion. I'm ecstatic about it!"

When the physical exam and test results were released to the public, her pregnancy was plastered all over the front pages of the newspapers. Many women's groups were also ecstatic. Kelli was making history again!

Kevin Powers called her on the phone. "I guess that definitely does it!"

"That's right!" replied Kelli.

"I'm sure you'll support the Party's choice. When is your baby due?"

"I'm not sure, probably in July. If all goes well, I'll have eight to ten weeks to help the candidate. Who do you want, Kevin?"

"I know your V.P. Hatfield wants it, but he's not in your league. We may have a wide open convention."

"That might make it more exciting."

"What does your husband have to say about all of this?"

"He's as happy as a lark and the kids are, too."

As soon as Kelli announced that she wouldn't be running for reelection, all sorts of candidates came out of the woodwork, on both sides of the aisle. It looked like the coming election was going to be a real interesting donnybrook. Some journalists felt that she should resign; because she was pregnant... others supported her.

V.P. Hatfield had many friends within the Party, and in the primary state elections and at the Democratic Convention; he was able to muster enough votes to get the nomination.

There were eight candidates on the Republican side of the aisle and the Senate Majority Leader, Preston Adams, was able to call in all his credits from his Party's constituents and just squeaked by at the Republican convention. The age issue was brought up because he was seventy-two years of age and Hatfield was only fifty-two.

In July, Kelli hit the newspapers again with a big splash. She had gained quite a bit of weight during her pregnancy and her latest ultrasound was dramatic. She had twins, a five-pound, four once boy and a four pound, three-ounce girl. The boy was named Thomas and the girl was named Tiffany. They were born by caesarean section and Kelli couldn't be happier. She stole the spotlight from the two candidates.

The personnel and White House staff were overwhelmed with what happened. Who would ever think that a nursery would be built in the White House for the President's newborn twins? It was.. in a hurry… and it had everything in it including two very vocal crying babies. Son Paul wasn't happy about the noisy additions to the family, but daughter Anne was in seventh heaven taking care of her baby brother and sister. She ran the show better than the two nannies and loved every minute of it.

The Presidential election was held in November and the country was ready for a change. Since Kelli wasn't running, Hatfield could not energize any great support. Preston Adams was elected by a slim margin. It was a generation gap election with the young voters voting for Hatfield and the older generation groups for Adams.

On inauguration day, Kelli told Preston she would be glad to help him at anytime if he wanted her help. And she said, "If you don't do a good job, I'll come back and run against you."

"I'll do a good job, Kelli," he replied. "You know I'll try my best, but you're a tough act to follow."